# STARFELL

## Willow Moss and the Lost Day

# STARFELL

## Willow Moss and the Lost Day

### DOMINIQUE VALENTE

#### ILLUSTRATED BY SARAH WARBURTON

HarperCollins *Children's Books*

First published in Great Britain by
HarperCollins *Children's Books* in 2019
HarperCollins *Children's Books* is a division of HarperCollins*Publishers* Ltd,
HarperCollins Publishers
1 London Bridge Street
London SE1 9GF

The HarperCollins website address is
www.harpercollins.co.uk

1

HARDBACK ISBN 978–0–00–830839–1
TRADE PAPERBACK ISBN 978–0–00–833505–2
PAPERBACK ISBN 978–0–00–830840–7

Printed and bound in England by CPI Group (UK) Ltd, Croydon CR0 4YY

**MIX**
Paper from
responsible sources

FSC
www.fsc.org

**FSC™ C007454**

For Catherine, who loved it first, to Helen for helping
to make a dream come true and to Rui for always
believing that it would

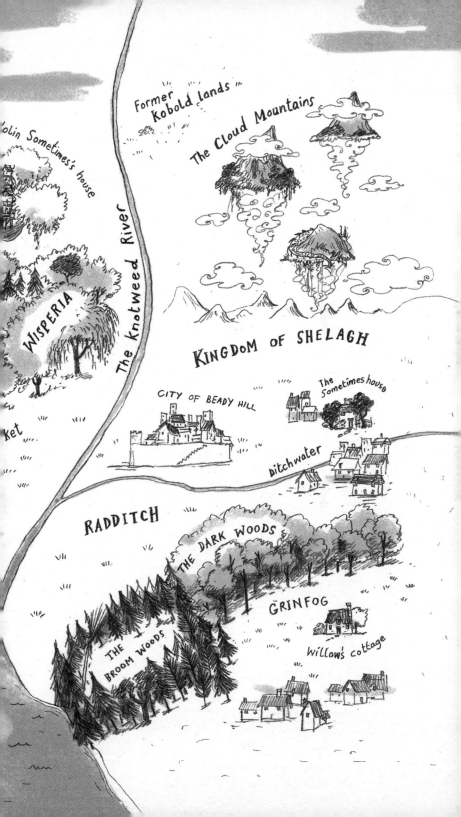

# 1

## The Girl Who Found Lost Things

Most people think being born with a magical power would be a bit of a dream come true. But that's only because they assume that they'd get *exciting* powers, like the ability to fly, become invisible or turn an annoying relative into a pig. They think *magic* is a big feast, where everything is laid out, ripe for the picking.

However, in the world of Starfell, not everyone who is lucky enough to have a bit of magic up their sleeve these days gets the really good bits – like, say, the triple-chocolate fudge cake. Some just get those wilted carrot sticks that no one really wanted to eat anyway. This seemed to be the unfortunate case for Willow Moss, the youngest and, alas, least powerful member of the Moss family.

Willow had received an ability that was, in most

9

people's opinions, a little more magical scrapyard than magical feast. Useful, but not in a snap, fizzle and bang sort of way. Not even a little snap, or a low sort of bang, though there was almost a fizzle, when you squinted.

Willow's power was in finding lost things.

Like keys. Or socks. Or, recently, old Jeremiah Crotchet's wooden teeth.

*That* hadn't been fun; the teeth had landed in Willow's outstretched palm, covered in gooey saliva from the mouth of Geezer, the Crotchets' ancient bullmastiff.

After the Crotchets paid Willow a spurgle – the standard rate since she was six – Willow decided that an increase was long overdue. She also made a vow from then on to keep a fisher's net with her at all times to catch the more unsavoury items she was likely to find.

So, while it wasn't exactly a profitable talent, it did put food on the table – usually a half loaf of bread most days. Which was something at least. Unless you compared it to her middle sister Camille's talent. Camille had recently lifted a plough, donkey still attached, off Garron Jensen, *with her mind.*

Yup . . . Camille's powers were *a bit* flashier.

It was at age six, when Willow's power had finally surfaced, that her father had explained to her that the world was made of different types of people. 'They're all necessary, all important. It's just that some attract a bit more attention than others. There are people like your mother, who commands respect the second she walks into a room. (The fact that she hears dead people speak helps with that a bit too.) Same with your sisters. And then there are people like me and *you.'*

Which hurt. Just a little.

Willow, despite her name, was short with long, stick-straight brown hair and brown eyes to match. She looked a lot like her father, while her sisters had inherited her mother's striking looks – tall with flowing black hair and green eyes that were described as 'emerald-hued'. Although Willow was pretty

certain no one in the Moss family had ever seen an emerald close up.

When Willow complained to Granny Flossy that she didn't look like her striking mother and sisters, Granny had harrumphed. She didn't have patience for vanity. She couldn't afford to with green hair. Granny Flossy had once been one of the best potion-makers in all of Starfell, but was now called 'Batty Granny' by most people due to a potion explosion in the mountains of Nach that had caused some rather interesting effects, one of which was the colour of her hair.

'Tsk, child. Your eyes may not be "emerald" like the others, but they're as good as, 'specially when it comes to spotting things that others don' seem to see,' she said with a sly grin, before she stashed a few of her dodgier potions beneath a loose floorboard in the attic that only Willow seemed to know about.

Granny Flossy was right about Willow spotting things other people seemed to miss. It had become a talent over the years. Like today, while she stood in the cottage garden in her usual position, looking at the small line of people that snaked round the low stone wall, all seeking Willow's help to find their misplaced possessions.

'I just can't seem to find them. I've looked everywhere . . .' said Prudence Foghorn from behind the open gate.

'Did you try on top of your head?' asked Willow.

'Oh my!' said Prudence, feeling the top of her head only to discover her missing rhinestone spectacles. 'Silly me,' she said with an embarrassed giggle before turning away.

'That'll be one spurgle,' said Juniper, Willow's oldest sister, coming out of the cottage and witnessing the exchange.

'But she didn't do any magic,' complained Prudence, eyes popping in surprise.

'She still found your glasses, didn't she? You got the same result that you came here for, didn't you? It's not her fault you're too blind to look in a mirror.' Juniper was relentless, and under her glare Prudence conceded and handed over the spurgle.

'I heard witches weren't meant to ask for money in the first place,' whined skinny Ethel Mustard from near the back of the queue. 'They're not meant to profit from their gifts,' she said rather piously, gimlet eyes shining.

Ethel Mustard, it has to be said, was the sort of

*13*

person who secretly wished that their village, Grinfog, had been granted Forbidden status by the king. This would ensure that people like Willow and her family – *magical people, really* – would have to go and live *Somewhere Else.*

'Who told you that?' said Juniper, rounding on Ethel, who appeared to shrink under Juniper's dark frown. 'When a carpenter makes you something, you pay him, don't you? My sister supplies you a service, so why would it be any different with her?'

'Well, because she's *not* like everyone else,' whispered Ethel, two high spots of colour appearing on her cheeks.

Juniper's eyebrows lowered. '*Well,*' she drawled, '**perhaps then you should pay her more?**'

There was collective grumbling from all around.

Juniper's power – besides getting money out of people – was in blowing things up. So no one grumbled too loudly. No one wanted to anger someone who could blow *them* up.

14

Willow sighed. She was planning on raising her price to a fleurie and a Leighton apple, but she wasn't convinced that using her scary sister to bully it out of people was the *best* way to go about it. It wasn't that she was overly fond of Leighton apples, but Wheezy the Jensens' retired show horse was. Willow passed the old horse every Thursday when she went to the market. The children from the village had labelled him Wheezy because every time he came trotting to the pasture his chest made asthmatic wheezes. Considering that he went to the trouble to come greet her, Willow liked to have his favourite treat.

'The trouble with you, Willow,' said Juniper, who Willow couldn't help noticing had failed to hand over the spurgle, 'is that you don't place enough value on your skills – such as they are.'

'Skills! What skills?' came Camille's mocking tones as she emerged from the cottage, dressed head to foot in a long black robe made of rich, shimmery material.

'Oh, you mean as a magical bloodhound?' She smirked. Ignoring Willow's protests, she turned to Juniper and said, 'Ready?' The two were heading off to join their mother for the Travelling Fortune Fair.

Willow closed her eyes and concentrated on breathing deeply. When she opened them she saw that her sisters had sped off down the lane, their black hair and cloaks flowing in their wakes.

Resignedly she turned back to her queue of customers and jumped.

The queue had vanished, and in its place stood a lone woman. She was tall and reed-thin, with black hair framing a pale, slender face marked by high arching eyebrows. She wore a long dusky gown with purple pointed boots, and an expression that made Willow's spine straighten before her brain could muster an objection.

The woman raised a brow and said, 'Good morning?'

'G-good morning . . . ?' managed Willow in response, wondering who the woman was.

There was a small part of Willow's mind that held its breath. It was the part that seemed to be listening to her knees, which had begun to shake, as if they knew a secret her head did not.

'Moreg Vaine,' said the woman with casual nonchalance, as if declaring yourself the most feared witch in all of Starfell was an everyday occurrence. Which, to be fair, for Moreg Vaine, it probably *was*.

'Oh dear,' said Willow, whose wobbling knees had proved correct.

Moreg Vaine's mouth curled up.

In years to come Willow would still wonder how it was possible that she had managed to keep her feet on the ground when a whisper would surely have knocked her over.

Yet never in Willow's wildest fantasies of meeting the infamous witch Moreg Vaine could she ever have imagined for a moment what happened next.

'Cup of tea?' suggested Moreg.

# 2

# A Question of Time

Willow followed Moreg Vaine into the cottage, staring in bafflement as the witch went about lighting the coal in the blackened stone fireplace, and filling the old dented teakettle with water. Moreg patted down her robe, withdrew a package and nodded to herself as she poured something into the pot.

'Hethal should do nicely,' she said, drumming a finger against her chin. Seeming to remember herself she said, 'Take a seat,' offering Willow a chair at Willow's own kitchen table.

Willow sat down slowly. Somewhere deep inside she clung to the faint hope that this was all just a dream, or perhaps the witch had come to the wrong house by mistake? Even so, her manners soon caught up with her and she mumbled, 'Er, Miss Vaine . . . I-I can do that if you'd like . . . ?'

Moreg waved her hand dismissively. 'No matter – I remember where everything is.'

Willow's mouth popped open in surprise. 'You do?'

Taking down two cups from the old wooden dresser, Moreg shrugged. 'Oh yes. It's been a long time, of course, but Raine and I go back many years.'

'You know *my mother?*'

Moreg placed a chipped blue mug decorated with small white flowers before Willow and sat down opposite with a dainty teacup for herself.

'Since we were young girls. Did she never mention it?'

Willow shook her head a bit too vigorously.

Willow knew, logically, that her mother – and she supposed *Moreg Vaine* – had once been a young girl, but it was a concept her brain couldn't fully grasp. Like trying to understand why anyone would willingly choose to spend their time collecting postage stamps. All she could manage was a polite, puzzled frown.

Moreg said offhandedly, 'It was a long time ago, I suppose, long before you were born. Like many of our people – magical people, that is – our families lived in the Ditchwater district. Your mother was great friends with my sister, Molsa, you see. As children they did

19

everything together, setting bear traps to catch the local hermit, holding tea parties with the dead, dancing naked in the moonlight . . . but things changed – they always do, and many of us have moved on . . . It's safer that way, and Molsa is gone now.' Moreg cleared her throat. 'Never mind that, though, drink your tea.'

'Um,' was all Willow managed in response, trying really hard NOT to picture her mother dancing naked in the moonlight.

Willow looked at the witch, then away again fast. Moreg's eyes were like razors. Willow's throat turned dry as she remembered one of the scarier rumours about the witch. And they were *all* rather scary to be sure. It was said that Moreg Vaine could turn someone to stone just by looking at them . . . Willow glanced at her mug and wondered, *Why IS she here? Making me tea?* She took a sip. It was good too. Strong and sweet, the way she liked it. And the cup was hers – one of the few items in the cottage that was. It stood alone among the haphazard collection of cups and saucers that bowed the Mosses' kitchen dresser.

She supposed that senior witches made it their business to know which mug was yours. *At some point I'm going to have to actually ASK her why she is here,*

Willow thought with dread. She took another sip of tea to stretch that moment out just *a little* longer.

*Maybe*, Willow wondered, *Moreg is here to visit Mum?* That seemed the most likely explanation.

Willow hadn't taken more than two sips before Moreg dashed her hopeful musings. She looked at Willow, with her eyes like deepest, blackest ink, and said rather worryingly, 'I need your help.'

Willow blinked. 'M-my help?'

Moreg nodded. 'It's Tuesday, you see. I can't quite put my finger on why or how . . . but I'm fairly certain that it's gone.'

'G-gone?'

Moreg stared. 'Yes.'

There was an awkward silence.

Willow stared at Moreg.

The witch stared back.

There seemed to be no other explanation. The witch must have gone *mad*. Granny Flossy said it happened to the best of them sometimes. She'd know, of course, having gone mad herself.

Some said Moreg Vaine lived alone in the Mists of Mitlaire, the entrance to the realm of the undead. Willow supposed that would be enough to drive

anyone round the bend. Mad and powerful seemed a rather dangerous combination, so she gave the witch a slightly nervous smile, hoping that she'd just misunderstood. 'Gone? The d-day?'

Moreg nodded, then got up and took the Mosses' Grinfog calendar from its peg behind the cottage door and handed it to Willow.

Willow looked.

She wasn't sure what she was meant to be looking at; she was half expecting to see that the week just skipped from Monday straight to Wednesday. She was mildly disappointed to find that it had not. Tuesday was still there. Along with the Leightons' advertisement for apple cider to cure all ailments.

'But it's still . . . ?'

Moreg nodded impatiently. 'It's there – yes – but look closely.'

Willow looked. Printed on each day of the calendar were fairs, village meetings, harvest schedules, phases of the moon and other events. Each day had at least one item – except Tuesday.

She frowned. 'But that could mean any—'

'—thing. Yes. I thought that too. But, still, I can't shake this feeling that it means some*thing*.

Something bad.' Moreg paused before explaining. 'Do you remember what you did on Tuesday?'

Willow frowned. She closed her eyes and for just a second a big moth-eaten purple hat with a long green feather sticking up jauntily to the side swam before her eyes, with Granny Flossy's face turning away from her, and for a moment she felt her stomach clench with fear. But then, just as fast as the image had appeared, it was gone, taking the momentary feeling of disquiet along with it.

She thought hard, the way you think about a dream that feels so real when you just wake up but is gone within seconds and is almost impossible to recall. On Monday she helped farmer Lonnis find his lease. Without it he would have lost his rights to grow oranges, but luckily Willow had been dispatched, and all was well with Lonnis Farms now – she'd got a whole bag of oranges for that. Then she'd come home and helped Granny Flossy to repot the grumbling Gertrudes. The sweet purple fruits were used for masking some of the nastier flavours from her potions (it didn't really work, just like most of Granny's potions didn't really work since her accident). On Wednesday she'd gone to the market – helping the

housewives of Herm find their misplaced household goods. Thursday, her mother left for the fair, and then it was today . . .

'Not really – I can't seem to remember what I did that day.'

Moreg nodded, then sighed. 'I was hoping it may be different, but it's the same with everyone I've spoken to – they seem to recall most of what they did this week, but Tuesday is a real blank.'

Willow bit her lip, hesitating. 'But isn't that . . . ?'

'Normal?' supplied Moreg, waving her hand dismissively. 'Yes, of course. Most people struggle to remember what they had for dinner the night before. Usually, though, if they put their minds to it, something will come up. But the thing is, when it comes to Tuesday, not a single person I have questioned can remember what happened. *Not even me.*'

Willow frowned. She had to admit that it was strange. 'How many people have you asked?'

Moreg gave her an appraising look. 'All of Hoyp.'

Willow's eyebrows shot up. That *was* surprising: an entire village. Okay, a small village that was really more like one long road, but still, that was around fifteen families at least.

Another thought occurred to her. She hesitated, but asked anyway. 'Why did you say *even me?*'

A ghost of a smile crossed Moreg's face. 'You're sharp – that's good. I meant only that it was strange, as it had never happened to me before.'

Willow was taken aback. 'You've never forgotten what you've done before?'

'Never.'

Willow's eyes popped. She didn't really know what to do with that information. She felt equal parts awe and dismay at the prospect.

Moreg changed the subject. 'I believe that you are a finder?'

Willow hesitated; she'd never been called that before. Mentally she cringed. The closest she'd ever come to being called that was when her sister Camille took to calling her 'Fetch' for a large portion of her childhood. She'd stopped that now. Mostly.

'Yes. Well. No. Not exactly. I mean . . . I find things . . . things that are lost.'

Moreg said nothing.

Willow filled the silence in a rush. 'I mean . . . I could find your keys if you lost them, but I don't think I could find an entire day . . . even if it was lost.'

25

Moreg raised a brow. 'But you could try, couldn't you?'

Willow considered. She could. There was nothing stopping her from at least *trying*. She took a deep, nervous breath, closed her eyes, and raised her arm to the sky, concentrated hard on Tuesday then –

'STOP THAT THIS INSTANT!' thundered Moreg, jumping out of her seat so fast she overturned her chair, which hit the flagstone floor with a deafening clatter. Willow gulped, while Moreg watched her lower her arm as if it were a dangerous viper. Clutching her chest, the witch took several sharp, shuddery breaths.

'SUCH A FRIGHT!' 'MY HEART!'

Willow's voice shook as she spoke in a tone trying its absolute best *not* to make an accusation. 'I don't understand – you asked me to . . . try?'

Moreg rubbed her throat, and after a moment her voice went back to almost normal, though there was a faint squeak if you listened closely enough.

'Q-quite right, quite right,' she repeated. 'Yes, I *did*. I do want you to try, just not quite *yet*. Dear Wol, no! Not without some kind of a plan first – we can't just go in and get it. One can only imagine the consequences . . .' she said with a violent shudder that she shook off. 'Bleugh!'

At Willow's frown Moreg explained. 'I believe,' she said, her black marble-like eyes huge, 'that had you succeeded in finding the missing Tuesday and brought it into our current reality, the result would almost certainly have been catastrophic – it's possible that the very structure of our universe would have split apart, creating a sort of end-of-days scenario . . .'

'Pardon?' asked Willow.

'I believe it may have **ended** the world.'

Willow sat back, heart jack-hammering in her chest. Finding out that she could have ended the world was, to say the least, a sobering thought.

27

Moreg, however, seemed back to normal.

'The thing is, until we know what happened we could just make things worse. Worse than it already is now, and right now it's about as bad as can be imagined.'

Willow frowned in confusion. 'What do you mean? I know it's not . . . um, great that Tuesday has gone missing, but it's not the end of the world, surely? It's just one day . . .'

*A day that no one seems to have missed anyway, so what was the harm, really?* thought Willow.

Moreg blinked. 'Actually, it might be the *end of the world* if we don't find it. **Whatever happened to last Tuesday may affect the very fabric of Starfell, causing it to unravel slowly, thread by thread.**'

Willow's mouth fell open dumbly as she gasped. She hadn't realised it could be that serious.

Moreg nodded. 'Which is why we will have to start at the beginning. We can't very well proceed until we know for sure what happened. Or, more importantly, why.'

She looked out of the window, frowning slightly, then blinked as if she were trying to clear her vision. 'There's someone I think we're going to need, someone who can help us . . . which might prove a little tricky

as we need to find him first.'

'Oh, why's that tricky?' asked Willow.

Moreg turned to look at her, a faint smile about her lips. 'He's an oublier, you see, one of the best in Starfell, no doubt, coming from a long line of them. The problem is that finding an oublier is almost impossible unless you know where to look.'

Willow looked blank. 'An ouble— A what?'

'An oublier. It's in the Old Shel, you see.' Which Willow had always taken to mean when words had more bits in it. Modern-day Shel was the language most people spoke in Starfell, apart from High Dwarf that is, but the latter was mostly because of all the colourful ways one got to swear. 'It's pronounced *oo-blee-hair*, or – as they are more commonly known today – forgotten tellers, people who see the past.'

'Like the opposite of a seer?'

Moreg drummed her chin with her fingers. 'Sort of—'

'Like my mother,' interrupted Willow, whose mother was a well-known seer, and took her travelling fair all across the kingdom of Shelagh telling fortunes.

Moreg seemed to have something stuck in her

throat because she answered with a strained voice. 'Er, yes, like your mother. Though most people who call themselves "seers" and say that they can see the future have no idea how it is really done, and often claim to have some connection to the "other side", to the dead, who supposedly let them know when things are about to occur,' she said with a disbelieving sniff. 'True seers are, of course, very rare. But they have been known to read patterns in the smallest events, allowing them to see possible versions of the future. For instance, if they see a particular flower blooming in winter when it usually blooms in spring they can work out that a typhoon is coming in the summer.'

Willow stared blankly.

Moreg continued, 'Unless they somehow encourage the last tree sparrow to build its nest before midnight on the spring equinox, for example. Do you understand?'

Willow made a kind of nod, mostly because it seemed like it was expected. But she didn't really understand *at all*.

Moreg continued, not noticing Willow's confusion. 'Forgotten tellers, on the other hand, read people's memories of the past, which come to them like visions when other people are around. They are, alas,

rather unpopular compared to seers, and have very few friends, as you can imagine . . .'

Willow was puzzled. 'Why's that?'

'Well, seers should be unpopular too. No one wants to be around someone who can predict their *death* . . . Yet so very few of them really *can* predict such things – so they make excellent friends as they always tell you just what you'd like to hear. Forgotten tellers, on the other hand, seldom, if ever, tell you what you'd actually *like* to hear. They tell things most people would prefer to forget, things you may wish to pretend never happened . . .'

Willow's eyes bulged. 'Really?'

Moreg nodded. 'Oh yes. Take poor old Hercule Sometimes, a powerful forgotten teller. He was found drowned in a well after he walked past the Duke of Dittany and embarrassed him in front of the captain of the king's army. The duke had been boasting that he had fantastic natural archery skills, and that the very first time he'd used a bow and arrow he'd hit the bull's-eye. Apparently Hercule stopped in his tracks, slapped his knee, started chortling and said, "You mean when you fell over backwards in a field after you'd released the arrow and poked a bull in the eye

with your bow?"' Moreg chuckled. 'See, he'd seen the duke's memory of the day and, well, the duke was less than impressed, as you can imagine . . .'

'But why did he tell the duke?' gasped Willow.

Moreg's lips twitched. 'Couldn't help himself – forgotten tellers see things as if they just happened. And they often blurt it out before they realise. They aren't stupid – they're just not always aware of what happens to them when they're having a vision. Making for rather awkward social situations. As a result very few oubliers have lived to tell their tales and have an alarming capacity for turning up buried beneath people's floorboards or at the bottom of wells. They often carry their own food for fear of being poisoned. They're deeply suspicious of gatherings of people, partly because they get flooded with other people's memories, and partly because the more visions they have the more chance they have of getting themselves into trouble by offending people. So the few that have survived are virtually hermits, who start running the minute they see anyone approaching . . .'

'Oh,' said Willow with a frown. 'How are we going to find one, then, if they're impossible to find?'

'Tricky, I said,' grinned Moreg. 'But not impossible, if you know where to start.'

'And you do?'

'Oh yes. I've found in life that sometimes it's useful to look back a little, to see when you need to go forward.'

'Huh?'

'We're going to visit his last known address.'

'Oh,' said Willow, blinking at the ominous use of 'we'.

'I think you may need to pack a bag.'

'Oh dear,' Willow whispered.

*Meanwhile, far away in a hidden stone fortress, where no magic had been able to penetrate for a thousand years, a figure stood alone in the tower and waited.*

Waited for the raven, and the message that could lead to his downfall, betraying his plans before he was ready to seize power.

There were shadows beneath his eyes; sleep was a tonic he could ill afford.

But no raven came this day. Just as it hadn't come the day before.

At last he allowed himself to breathe a sigh of relief; at last he allowed himself to believe. It had worked.

He put the box inside his robes, keeping it close to his heart. It had done its job well. Never again would he let the witch get the better of him.

He left the tower, and found his faithful followers waiting on the winding stone staircase for the news. 'She can't remember?' asked one, his face dark, hidden behind the hood of his robe. 'Does that mean she won't be coming?'

He gave a low, mirthless laugh. 'Oh, she will. I have no doubt of that. But this time I will be ready.'

## 3

* The Monster from Under the Bed

W illow spent the next quarter of an hour trying *not* to picture the look on her father's face when he got home from his job as a farm manager for Leighton Apples and found her gone. Moreg, meanwhile, explored the Mosses' 'fascinating cottage garden' in an attempt to give Willow a moment to pack in privacy.

In her small bedroom, which she shared with Camille, Willow took down Granny Flossy's old green shaggy-hair carpetbag from atop the cupboard; it was made from the long hairs of a Nach mountain goat. Willow had often wondered if it was age that had turned it green, or if there really were green mountain goats . . .

Willow tried to think of what she might need.

She'd never spent the night away from the cottage

before, not even to go to one of her mother's travelling fairs. She'd somehow always been too young or, when she was old enough, too established as the 'sensible one' – which translated as 'the one who was better suited to look after her father and Granny Flossy'.

Not that she minded looking after Granny. They looked after each other really. The two had been a pair since she'd come to live with them the year Willow turned five. Willow's father was sometimes a bit embarrassed by his formerly famous mother, whose potions had once been highly sought commodities, but which now mostly exploded in clouds of coloured smoke that left rat tails on the ceiling.

He tried to forbid her from making them, and tried locking away her supplies. He didn't seem to notice how Granny Flossy's shoulders slumped whenever he reprimanded her, or how much it hurt her when he treated her like a child. Willow knew, though, just like she knew where he hid the key. It was why Granny brewed most of her potions in secret in the attic when he was gone. Willow and Granny spent most of their days there together, with Willow trying her best to ensure that Granny's potions didn't blow up the roof again. And even though Camille said that the pair were perfectly matched because Willow's magic was rather humdrum and Granny's was rather disastrous, she didn't mind. Somehow that made things better, not worse.

But now, as a result of being at home with Granny Flossy all these years, her 'worldly' experience was rather limited, to say the least, and she had absolutely no idea what someone was supposed to take on a potentially dangerous adventure. Moreg had told her that they might be gone for a week, or two, if everything went according to plan, and that it was best for the moment not to say anything about what they were really doing in case her parents came tearing after them (which might make saving the world harder than it needed to be).

Willow's sensible side had come up with a few objections. Like, why, for instance, she had the questionable luck of being home alone when the most feared witch in all of Starfell came knocking? Or the fact that this plan meant that no one knew where she was going, or, more importantly, who she was with . . .? A rather *fearsome* who as it turned out.

But 'no' didn't seem a word Moreg Vaine often heard. So Willow had said yes, partly because she

was a bit too afraid to say no, but also because it sounded like a pretty serious problem, so shouldn't she try to help . . . if she could? But mainly she'd said yes because hadn't she always secretly wished for something like this? Even that morning while she was hanging up her sisters' underwear on the line she had wished that she could go somewhere *exciting* just once, somewhere beyond the Mosses' cottage walls, and do something that didn't involve finding Jeremiah Crotchett's teeth. But, as Granny Flossy always said, wishes are dangerous things, especially when they come true. Which was why, now, she was a bit worried that this was a bit more adventure than she'd bargained for . . .

Willow looked at her belongings and frowned. She probably needed more than just an extra pair of socks?

It took her another five minutes to gather everything she might need, which coincidentally amounted to everything she owned:

✳ *Her second dress, pond green* – previously belonging to Juniper and taken up rather haphazardly by her Granny Flossy, so that it bubbled around her feet like a balloon

* *Three pairs of thick bottle-green wool socks*

* *A large, rather lumpy fisherman's jersey of indeterminate colour, mostly pea green* – a hand-me-down from her father

* *An enormous, and very old, slightly mouldy-looking khaki-green nightdress* – once belonging to Granny Flossy

* *One pale-blue scarf dotted throughout with small white horseshoes* – still belonging to her sister Camille

Briefly she wondered why almost everything she owned was a rather unfortunate shade of green. She then stood thinking for a minute, her fingers drumming her chin, trying to make up her mind: should she, or shouldn't she? Then she knelt down, and after a bit of scrambling she pulled out the monster who lived under the bed, clasping him firmly by his long tail. This was to his absolute horror, which sounded like this: 'Oh **no!** Oh, **me** greedy **aunt! A pox** on **you** from **all** of the **kobolds!**' and she put him alongside her worldly belongings.

39

'Monster' was a bit of a stretch. Oswin was, in fact, a kobold, a species that only *just* fell into the classification of monster. But it was best not to tell Oswin this as he was very proud of his monster heritage.

Through groggy slits that exposed luminous orange eyes that hadn't seen daylight for several weeks Oswin was glaring at her now. His lime-green fur was turning a ripe pumpkin colour in his outrage and his bright green-and-white striped tail electrified with indignation.

'**Wot** choo **go** and do that **for?** Grabbing **peoples** by the **tail?** Is that any **way** to treat a **body?** No **respect . . .** and **me** being the last **kobold** and **all!**' he muttered darkly. Then he scratched a shaggy ear with a long, slightly rusty claw and grumbled, '**I 'ave 'alf** a mind to

leave . . . Specially after **I got** you them awfully resistible feet **thingamababies,** which you *never* even **fanked** me for,' he pointed out with a deep hard-done-by sniff.

Oswin was always a bit cross, so Willow ignored this.

The 'thingamababies' that he referred to were her next-door neighbour Mrs Crone-Barrow's ancient, rather dead-looking bunny slippers. Willow had made the mistake of muttering one night that her toes were cold, so Oswin had gone next door and prised the prehistoric slippers from the old woman's sticky, corn-crusted feet with a butter knife. Willow had woken up to the feeling of something warm, wet and icky attached to her feet, followed very closely by the sound of her own screaming when she realised what it was. She still shuddered at the memory.

Despite this, there was the faint, *very faint*, chance Oswin might come in handy on an adventure thought Willow. He was really good at spotting magical ability, as well as detecting lies, and his thick kobold blood allowed him to resist most forms of magic. He was also her only friend, and who would remember to feed him when she was gone?

41

Oswin, despite his threat, had made no attempt to leave and was now taking care of some morning monster ablutions: checking his fur for any stray bugs and polishing his teeth with a corner of Willow's bedcover. In fact, Oswin had been threatening to leave the relative comfort beneath Willow's bed ever since Willow first caught him three years ago. 'Caught' being the operative word, like an infection.

Willow had been called to the Jensens' farmhouse to deal with a case of a missing monster, wondering on the way over why the Jensens would want to *find* a monster . . . She decided not to think about it too much because, as her father always said, spurgles don't grow without fertiliser. But when she arrived and Mrs Jensen pointed to the stove, squealing, 'It's in there . . .!' Willow had been a little confused.

'What's in there?'

'The monster, of course.'

Willow had frowned. 'But, Mrs Jensen,' she'd replied, 'I can't deal with monsters!'

'You have to – you're a witch and . . . he's lost . . . Isn't that what you do, find things?'

'But . . . how can he be lost if he's right *there*?'

It turned out that the Jensens knew he was a lost

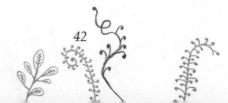

monster because Oswin had told them so shortly before he took up refuge in the stove. He refused to come out or to tell them where he was from for that matter. Later Willow would find out that this was a sore point, as he and his fellow kobolds had been banished from their home and scattered throughout Starfell due to a bit of thievery on the part of his aunt Osbertrude.

But Willow hadn't known any of *that* when she'd taken him from the Jensens' stove. She'd figured that if he really was 'lost', it couldn't hurt to try 'finding' him with her magic, using these precise words:

'I Summon the lost MONSTER currently residing in the Jensens' stove in Grinfog the kingdom of Shelagh, Starfell.'

It didn't hurt to be precise about such things just in case there were any other Jensens in any other parts of the world who also had lost monsters to contend with.

And Oswin had arrived into her outstretched arms with an orange plop. He was the size of a large and fluffy tabby cat, but one who glowered at her with cat-like fury. In fact, if you didn't know better, and you

were really quite stupid, you might mistake Oswin for a cat. To be sure, there were the pointed ears, the fluffy fur and the very stripy tail. He even (to his shame) had white paws, which made him look very tabby-like indeed. All *cat-tastic* really, except that he was green (when he wasn't cross, which was seldom), with very sharp monstery claws, the rather persistent smell of boiled cabbage, the stealing, the ease with which kobolds got offended, and the unfortunate truth that occasionally, when they were offended *enough*, they exploded. Which isn't great when they live under your bed. Oh, and the fact that he could talk – you don't get many tabby cats that can chat.

And once Oswin was 'found' he was determined to stay that way . . . choosing to stay with Willow from then on and showing his appreciation for his new home under Willow's bed by bringing her 'presents' from the neighbours. Which wasn't good for business. Especially if your clients found out that the person who found their lost things also seemed to be the one who took them in the first place.

Willow cleared her throat. 'Listen, Oswin, apparently Tuesday has gone missing . . . and we are going to help Moreg Vaine to find it.' Then, because

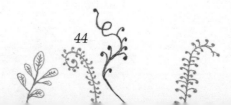

she felt that perhaps it was the right thing to do, she added, 'Er . . . you may want to pack a bag.'

Oswin turned tangerine; his eyes bulged to the size of tennis balls. **'Wot? We?'** His catty lips silently mouthed the words **'Moreg Vaine'** and his fur-covered body turned from carroty orange to a rather ill-looking shade of green like pea soup. **'Wot choo go and sign us up for a rumble with a madwoman for? Vicious witch, she eats peoples! She pickles children in ginger! Makes candles with yer earwax! And she blew up me cousin Osloss when he found 'imself in 'er pantry! Don't even think about it! I aren't going, *nohow, no way*! Staying right here ... I's got me a duty to stay as the last kobold anyhow,'** he said, glowering at Willow, his claws digging into the bedcover in stubborn revolt.

Willow sighed, then snatched him by the tail once more, and shoved him into the hairy carpetbag. 'Never mind all that,' she said dismissively, ignoring his hissing and muttering. She knew that kobolds blew up regularly, with or without a witch's help, and usually survived relatively unscathed. 'You're coming; now stop your grumbling.'

It was a *little* worrying, though, that rumours of Moreg Vaine even terrified the monster population.

Oswin sat in the bag with a huff, muttering darkly while Willow turned to the task at hand. The blue horseshoe scarf.

Would she *need* it? Was it necessary? Or was that really beside the point?

It was pretty, expensive and didn't actually belong to her. It belonged to her middle sister, Camille, who had received it from one of her many admirers. Knowing that Camille would be furious when she saw the scarf gone gave Willow a grim satisfaction that only those with older siblings understood. So she packed it in the bag along with everything else, closed her bedroom door and set the hairy bag down on top of the kitchen table with a thud (to Oswin's outrage). She decided at the last minute to add a half loaf of bread and her mug.

Then, fighting mounting panic, she scribbled her father a note:

Dear Dad,

~~Tuesday has gone missing~~

~~The witch Moreg has asked for my help~~

~~The witch Moreg has need of my skill — yes,~~ *really*

She scribbled over her first attempt and discarded it in the wastebasket when she remembered that honesty wasn't what they were going for. Not that he would believe her anyway . . . Then she tried again.

Dear Dad,

I've gone to help Mum and the girls at the travelling fair, sorry.

There is half a roast chicken in the icebox, and a loaf of bread under the tea towel.

If I'm not back in a week, please visit Wheezy for me. He likes the red Leighton apples, and won't be fooled by the green gumbos.

Love,

Willow

Leaving the note on the kitchen table, she tried not to think of what her father would say when he got home. Or what he would do to her when he realised that she wasn't with her mother and sisters at the travelling fair. There was no point in thinking about it.

Borrowed trouble. That's what her dad called it. He always said that the god Wol provided enough daily things to worry about and there was no use borrowing tomorrow's troubles as well. Though Willow doubted he'd appreciate her using his own logic against him.

Green hairy bag in hand, she whispered a warning to Oswin to keep quiet or she'd hand him over to Moreg Vaine for her ginger pickling, and with slightly trembling knees she closed the cottage door.

'Ready?' asked Moreg, who eyed the bag with some surprise, though she didn't comment.

Willow definitely didn't feel ready.

# 4

## The Portal Pantry

✳

As Willow followed the witch down the lane, leaving the cottage behind, there was a small part of her that wished one of her sisters – preferably Camille – would walk past just then. She thought how nice it would be to tell her that the most revered witch in all of Starfell needed *her* help.

But of course they passed no one. They walked along the winding dirt road that led away from Grinfog and its rolling fields and orchards. It forked left towards the shadowy woods that loomed on the horizon – woods that Willow had always been encouraged to stay out of.

'This way,' said Moreg, and Willow bit her lip nervously before she followed. Looking over her shoulder, she saw Wheezy, the Jensens' retired show horse, standing forlornly in his field down in the valley with his purple wool blanket on his flanks.

She supposed dismally, her knees trembling, that of course the witch would go through the dark woods rather than through the main roads that led out of Grinfog. From the slightly shaking carpetbag in her hands she could tell that Oswin was thinking the same thing.

As she turned to follow the witch into the woods a raven circled above their heads, making a strange, haunting cry. In the distance more ravens appeared. Willow couldn't hide a shudder, but Moreg looked up and smiled as if they were all old friends. Catching sight of Willow's face, the witch said, 'You know, a group of ravens are often called an "unkindness of ravens", but I prefer the less well-known term, a conspiracy.'

Willow frowned, her eyes following the birds as they circled. A conspiracy didn't sound much better. As she stared she saw one particular bird edge closer to Moreg; it looked different to the others, as if one of its wings was made of ink or smoke. Before Willow could comment, Moreg held up one long slim finger, and the bird vanished with a rapid beat of its black wings. Willow swallowed, eyeing Moreg warily. Had she made the bird disappear with a simple lift of a finger?

'Come on,' said Moreg almost nonchalantly. 'We'll stop a bit later for the night.'

As Willow followed the witch she thought about some of the other rumours she'd heard about Moreg over the years – like that she kept ravens, and that they carried her beneath Starfell into Netherfell so that she could dance with the dead. She darted a glance at Moreg and thought about asking if any of *that* was true, but then, catching sight of the witch's face, she changed her mind just as fast.

There was so much, though, that she did want to know. Like . . . did the witch really live in the Mists of Mitlaire – the fog that drove most people insane? Did she have several magical abilities as some had said? Or was that just a rumour, like the one Oswin had told her about the witch pickling children in ginger . . . which she still hoped was untrue.

They had been walking for nearly a mile through deep, dark woods, the air smelling of pine and moss and the cold and damp inching along Willow's toes, when Moreg slowed down. 'We'll be heading to the city of Beady Hill in the morning,' she said.

'It was the last known address of the forgotten teller we need, but it's some distance away – so we'll need a bit of help getting there.'

Willow wondered if she meant that they needed to catch a coach. But she had hoped that just maybe her adventure with Moreg would involve a bit of broom flying . . . so she dared to ask, 'Um, you . . . erm, don't want to fly?'

Moreg stared at her and Willow felt her cheeks burn slightly. But then the witch nodded. 'I would. I had a flying carpet for a while – quite rare, you know. A three-seater, once belonging to a Tetan king, I believe, but that's long gone now. Flew away right off the line, no doubt furious that it had been washed. Old carpets can be quite tetchy. Ordinarily I don't do brooms. I've never found one I really liked – it's such a stereotype, if you ask me, witches and brooms . . . Same with the hat. Never wear one if I can help it.'

Willow supposed that when she thought 'witch' a picture of a broomstick did float into her mind. Although, admittedly, the few witches she had met only owned a broom that did nothing more remarkable than sweep, but she had hoped that Moreg Vaine would

be the exception. After all, she was *Moreg Vaine.*

'I've always wanted to try a flying broom,' admitted Willow, who'd long wished for one of her own, and couldn't help feeling a little disappointed. If ever there was a time for a flying broom, surely saving the world was *it.*

Moreg looked at her, shrugged and said, 'Well, I suppose time is of the essence, and we are going past Radditch in any case . . .'

Willow blinked. Radditch . . . Something tugged at the corner of her mind. Weren't the people there known for something? Something to do with making things fly? A faint curl of hope expanded in her chest. Was the witch saying what she thought?

'So, despite my misgivings, I think we'll have to get some brooms, yes.' Moreg didn't look all that happy about it, though. 'First thing in the morning.'

Willow let out a small whoop of glee, and did a little jig, which made Oswin huff inside the carpetbag. She schooled herself fast when Moreg blinked at her in surprise.

'Um,' said Willow, clearing her throat self-consciously. 'Oh, okay, if you really think that's best.'

*

Dusk was setting as, sometime later, Willow and Moreg entered a fragrant wood. They walked on until they came across a small clearing covered in purple clover, where Moreg told her they'd be stopping for the night. 'We'll make an early start to Radditch tomorrow.'

Despite the promise of acquiring flying broomsticks, Willow was grateful to rest for the night. Her feet were sore, and she was tired and hungry. She set her carpetbag down, and then did a double-take when she saw what Moreg was doing. Seemingly, from out of nowhere, the witch had whipped out a large cast-iron pot, which she placed over an odd violet-hued flame that was suspended in mid-air. 'I hope you like nettle stew – it shouldn't take too long.'

'H-how did you do that?' exclaimed Willow.

Moreg waved a palm distractedly while testing the stew with a wooden spoon, and muttering, 'Needs salt, definitely.' She patted the front of her cloak, reached inside, and withdrew a small ceramic pot from which she took a pinch of salt and sprinkled it into the pot. Then, seeing Willow's bemused stare, she said quite nonchalantly, 'Oh this? Been cooking all day.'

Willow blinked. *What?*

Moreg, however, looked unfazed. 'Oh, how rude of me. Would you like a seat?' She asked, proceeding to pull out a folded blue chair from within her cloak. She sprung it open and offered it to Willow, who took it rather bemusedly. She watched as Moreg took more things from within the cloak's folds – including a small green table, and two knives, forks, plates and purple glasses. Moreg patted her cloak, rolled her eyes heavenward, and sighed deeply, 'I must have left the good wine in my other cellar – looks like we'll be roughing it. Just the rynflower cider for us. I suppose we'll survive,' she said, pulling out a small jug with a doubtful expression.

Willow stared. *Her other cellar?* How on Starfell did the witch manage to keep all of that in one cloak? And manage to walk? The obvious answer was of course magic. But that was a broad answer, and magic, as far as Willow knew, didn't work the way people believed it should. Not any more, not since it was nearly ripped away a thousand years before during the war started by the Brothers of Wol, a religious order who tried to rid Starfell of magic because they believed – and, alas, still did to this day – that people born with magical abilities were unnatural, and that

their bodies were possessed by evil. The battle resulted in what was known as the Long War. The old witches and wizards gathered together their best spells to fight them, but they were stolen, and the Brothers of Wol killed thousands of witches and wizards, destroyed enchanted forests and burned all the spell scrolls they could to try to rid the world of magic.

But they had failed. They didn't know the truth. Magic never dies – it simply waits until we are ready for it. When centuries had passed it trickled back, ever so slowly, into Starfell.

But this magic wasn't like the magic from before. It had changed. Perhaps it had learnt. Maybe it worried that if it gave too much it would be ripped away again. When it did at last come slowly slinking back, it did so cautiously, only gifting a few with tiny slithers of itself.

These days people who had a magical ability usually didn't have more than one, yet they still called themselves witches and wizards. But they were not like the old witches and wizards from before, known now as the old magicians of Starfell, who didn't just have a singular magical ability – they had many. Magic in the world was different then too; it

ran freely through the land, through the streams and rivers, mountains and glades. And some of the most powerful magicians back then harnessed this magic through powerful spells.

But that world was long gone. Just like those old powerful spells that the magicians had gathered together to fight the Brothers of Wol, which had passed into myth as the Lost Spells of Starfell. Today few witches and wizards could perform even the simplest spells, and, as far as Willow knew, no one with a magical ability could do what Moreg seemed to be doing now, which was to use magic like it was available on tap.

'How do you keep all of that with you?' Willow asked.

Moreg, who had just taken a fancy purple cushion out of her cloak, looked up and shrugged. 'Oh . . . I don't. I believe in travelling light really.'

Willow's mouth fell open. 'B-but then how do you have all this stuff?' she exclaimed, looking from the table to the stewing pot and folding chairs in disbelief.

Moreg cocked her head to the side. 'I don't, not really – it's a portal cloak. I had it made in Lael, so now I have access to my store cupboard, cellar and kitchen at home – very useful, I can tell you.'

'A portal *cloak*?'

Moreg dished up the thick, hearty stew, handed Willow a heavy stoneware plate and sat down opposite her on her own fold-up chair, plumping the purple cushion, which she put behind her back. 'Lousy lumbago,' she muttered. Then seeing that Willow was still waiting for an answer to her question she said, 'You know what a portal is?'

Willow thought. 'It's like a door to somewhere else?'

'Exactly, except it doesn't need to be a door, it can even be a—'

'A cloak,' breathed Willow in wonder.

Moreg smiled. 'Quite.'

'Wow.'

'It has its uses. Not all of us have your skill – anything you need summoned like that.' She snapped her fingers. 'That's truly something.'

Willow shrugged. 'Only if it's lost, though. It's a bit

annoying. I can't summon my own toothbrush unless I've lost it first . . . and leaving things at home doesn't count as lost.' She ran her tongue over her teeth and sighed. She had, in fact, forgotten her toothbrush.

Moreg tapped her nose conspiratorially, then winked. 'But you work around that . . . don't you?'

Willow's mouth fell open in surprise. How did she know? Could she really read minds, like some people thought?

Willow did 'lose' things that might be useful later. You couldn't be too deliberate or else the magic wouldn't work, but if, for example, you placed a spare bit of change in a pocket that you 'forgot' had a hole in it, well, it could save you running home for your wallet on market day. (Incidentally this had caused Prudence Foghorn to appear momentarily impressed the other day, before she asked after Willow's more *remarkable* sister Camille.) Sometimes it helped you to plan ahead when you wanted to 'accidentally' lose a rather lumpy old quilt that had been made from several of your granny's hairy dresses. You'd have to forget on washday, just, for example, while you were hanging it up to dry, that there was a gale-force wind forecast. But who knew when you might need to

summon the warmth of an additional quilt?

Moreg laughed, but she looked no less scary. 'It's what I'd do myself . . . that's the secret to being a good witch. Always be a step ahead if you can. *Practical makes perfect.*'

Willow frowned. 'I thought it was practice?'

Moreg scoffed. 'That's just for people who like to waste time. Who needs to practise something when they can be prepared the first time around?' she said, tapping her cloak.

That seemed true enough.

A small, rather grumpy voice from within Willow's hairy bag mumbled, '**An**' oo 'elps 'er to lose **fings** so she **can** find it? Jes like a witch **to take all the** credit. **Din't** she say jes the **other** day that she wished she **could** lose her fisher's net . . . sayin' that it would **be a bit more featrical** when the time came for **her** to find people's lost thingamababies she could **summons it** and ketch **it**? So din't I frow it into **Lost** Man's Lake where **fings disappear** never **ter be** seen again . . . Not **that she** cares. Oh **no**! Stick me **in a bag** made of 'air, only the last kobold and all . . . not like I *wanted* any of the stew, **nohow.**'

A loud silence followed this. Moreg looked at Willow. Willow looked at Moreg.

*Then.* 'What was that?' asked the witch.

'That,' sighed Willow, 'was nothing . . .'

The witch raised a brow and Willow hastened to add, 'That you would care to know about. Trust me.'

Witches for the most part aren't stupid, so Moreg didn't press it. But she did say rather loudly, 'A witch's business is none but her own. However, my cellar and pantry are off bounds . . . not unless *a kobold* wants to be turned into a full tabby cat.'

There was a distinctive gasp from within the bag. Willow snorted.

After helping Moreg do the dishes (Moreg, of course, had hot water and a tin basin ready), Willow climbed into her camp bed, and even though it was her first night away from the cottage in her whole life she fell instantly asleep, despite Oswin's grumblings. **'Why** she 'ave to **take** it that **far?** Turn me into a **common cat!** Jes because I's a **monster** don' mean I **don'** 'ave feelings . . . *sniff.'*

# 5

## The Broom-makers

The next morning, after they'd packed up their sleeping bags, and Willow had attempted to brush her teeth with her finger, they came across a rather unwelcome sight. Standing with their backs to Willow and Moreg by a clump of tall trees were a large gaggle of around twenty men wearing distinctive brown and gold robes.

Moreg held up a hand, just as a faint **'Oh no'** came from within Willow's carpetbag.

'Brothers of Wol,' she said softly. Her face turned to marble, like she was annoyed, then gestured for Willow to go back the way she'd come.

Willow gave a silent gasp. The Brothers of Wol still had a rather archaic view of witches – mostly that they thought the best way to deal with them was by burning them at the stake. The Brothers lived in

Wolkana – a hidden fortress that no magical being could find, let alone enter. And when they weren't there, plotting and scheming, you could guarantee they were out causing trouble for people with magic in their veins. Such as trying to ensure that no witches or wizards entered Forbidden areas. These were towns and cities that had decided that they would prefer not to have magical residents on their doorstep.

When magic had at first begun to trickle back into the world, families like Willow's and Moreg's had been forced to live in enclosed settlements like Ditchwater. Gradually things had changed; as magical people grew in number, a compromise was needed. Magical people agreed not to use their abilities on people without their permission, as well as to only live in areas where they were welcome.

Some moved away to more accepting pockets of Starfell over the years, but they never forgot the shadow of persecution, which was why some witches and wizards – like *Moreg Vaine*, for instance – kept the location of their home a firm secret, vowing never to have to answer to anyone ever again.

'We could fight them,' said Moreg, who appeared for a moment to consider it. 'I could get rid of them now . . .'

Willow swallowed, hoping the witch didn't mean what she thought she meant. She was finding the nerve to ask when Moreg shook her head, her eyes going hazy for a second, before she blinked. 'But not quite yet, no . . . She'll need it, so this is best, yes.'

Willow stared blankly at Moreg. 'Er, sorry?'

Moreg seemed to snap out of her reverie, gave a

small nod, and said, 'Back the way we came, I think. We can go round, and still get to Radditch that way.'

They crept backwards slowly, careful not to alert the Brothers to their presence.

It was some time before Willow's heartbeat slowed down. She was wildly relieved, however, that the witch had decided *not* to fight around twenty witch-hating men.

The closer they got to Radditch, the less Willow thought of the Brothers, and the more she wondered about the people they were going to meet. Broom-makers. She couldn't believe that she was finally going to see brooms that actually flew!

'All the best broom-makers are Mementons,' said Moreg. 'Which, as you know, means we need to remember one important thing . . .'

Willow swallowed, waiting for the warning. From within the carpetbag there was a faint **'Oh no,'** from Oswin.

She'd heard the stories of Mementons – mostly from Granny Flossy. They were part elf, somewhat spirrot, and sort of human, like a distant cousin no one liked to mention (but, if you squinted, you could see the resemblance, almost). They were over nine

feet tall, very hairy and slim, and had an aversion to cutting their toenails beyond seven inches, believing that's where they kept their power. It was certainly why others kept their distance.

'We mustn't stay for lunch.'

Willow frowned. 'Oh? Why?'

Moreg shrugged. 'Because they take hours at every meal – and we really need to keep moving.'

She saw the look of incredulity Willow shared with the tops of Oswin's narrowed eyes, which were peeking out of the carpetbag, and scoffed, 'Oh, you're thinking about that silly thing about them *eating humans*? I wouldn't worry. That went out of fashion some time ago . . .'

Willow gulped. That was a rumour she could have done without knowing.

By mid-morning they had entered a wood filled with trees that towered above their heads. Through the branches she glimpsed the broom-makers at work and gasped. They were incredibly tall, like slim walking and moving trees themselves, and they were all hard at work. They had long curly nails, which matched the colour of their hair. Some were strange electric

67

colours, like the brightest blue and green, which glinted in the dappled forest light. As Willow watched she saw that there were hundreds of workstations with different Mementons all involved in various stages of broom construction.

News of their arrival spread quickly. Within seconds a rather short Mementon (at just below nine feet) came forward to greet them. Willow's first impression was *BLUE*. Followed quickly by *HAIR*.

He had very bright and very wild, bushy blue hair that trailed from his head, met at his triangular beard and seemed to end somewhere by his waist.

'Moreg!' greeted the Mementon, blinking rapidly. 'Er, what brings you here?' he asked a little nervously, darting a look at Moreg, who as far as Willow could see was trying her best to appear friendly. She wasn't frowning at least.

The Mementon's eyes were strange. They were deep dark blue, with white flecks in them, so that it looked like small chips of the night sky full of stars. Willow wondered if he saw things differently with eyes like that.

Moreg introduced Willow to Chopak and said, 'Well, we need your help, you see; speed is of the essence, and we're in the market for two of your brooms.'

Chopak's pointy ears shot up in shock. '*You* – you're looking for a broom?' It sounded like he couldn't believe his ears.

Moreg sighed. 'I'm afraid so.'

Which seemed a little rude . . . but neither of them *dared* point that out to the witch.

Willow couldn't help marvelling at all that she saw. Seeing this, Chopak, who was at heart a born salesman, said, 'Come with me, I'll give you the tour.' They followed after him through the Broom Woods.

'That's the Twigging Depot – mostly suitable for the young ones,' he said, pointing a curling fingernail at a group of around twelve Mementons. Willow watched as a Mementon with bright ginger hair and nails to match tied up a bunch of twigs the size of a

small boulder with what looked like yarn on a large trestle table.

'Delicate work, see – suitable to their small fingers,' said Chopak, holding up his own sausage-like digits.

From within the bag Willow heard a faint mutter. **'Little 'uns?** Little 'uns, 'airy nutter! **Them** curly-clawed beasts are the **exact** opposite of *little*!'

'Shhh,' hissed Willow, giving the bag a little shake. The truth was, as friendly as these Mementons appeared, while they might have given up on humans, she wasn't sure if a kobold might not actually find itself as dinner . . .

'That's Assembly,' said Chopak, continuing. 'Self-explanatory really – that's where they are put together.' He pointed to a small area where a group of Mementons were carefully attaching the twig bundles to the broom handles. 'That's Strimming,' he said as they passed a group of very tall and thin-looking Mementons, who were examining brooms parked in mid-air from all angles, making adjustments here and there. 'We try to keep it down here, as they need the quiet,' he said in a whisper.

They walked past on tiptoes. 'And here –' he said, as they came to the heart of the dark woods – 'is where

the real magic happens; this is Awakening, where the broom comes to life . . . and tells you what it will become.'

There was a still quality to the air, as if it were waiting for something.

'They tell you?' asked Willow in surprise.

There was only one other Mementon present, a female with sleek auburn hair that flowed to her waist. The nails on her hands and feet were green, which matched her very large, luminous eyes.

'My wife,' whispered Chopak, 'Ybaer.' Ybaer was concentrating on the important task at hand, and he carried on whispering, so as not to disturb her. 'We call this the Spark – when the broom touches the hands of an Awakener it releases the magic – telling the broom-maker what type of broom it will become. You see, like people, wood has a personality and no broom is exactly the same as another.'

Ybaer's long fingers slid along the sapling, which lifted slowly into the air. After some time a very faint blue outline shone all around it.

Chopak explained. 'When it glows blue like that it's a Stealth.'

'A Stealth?' asked Willow, her eyes reflecting the

glow from the broom.

'Yes, while no two brooms are exactly the same, they tend to have one dominant personality trait – like people. Some people are reserved, some confident, some exacting . . .' Chopak said, eyeing Moreg. He cleared his throat, and then continued. 'In the same way a broom's dominant personality lends itself to different uses. Brooms tend to be Racers, Stealths, Torques or Jaunters. Racers are for those covering long-distance terrain and requiring a bit of speed; a Stealth is best for those who would prefer to pass unnoticed. Torques offer a rocket-like getaway, and Jaunters are for those who enjoy a Sunday-afternoon sort of glide. There are the rare few that combine their qualities. You can get weird combinations, though, just like people. We had a Jaunter-Racer once, a very bumpy stop-start ride. It reminded me of an old racing horse who occasionally remembered his victorious youth!'

Ybaer turned now to face them and gave a small bow in greeting. She didn't seem that surprised that Moreg Vaine was there. In fact, it was as if she were expecting her.

'Moreg,' she said, nodding, her green eyes wise. 'I

wondered if you'd come to us. Strange things have been happening; I have been reading the signs . . .'

'As have I,' agreed Moreg. 'What have you seen?'

'Brooms that have appeared, which none of us remember making – and yet they appear to be some of our best yet.'

Chopak nodded. 'We've tried replicating the process but without knowing what was done to begin with . . . it's impossible.'

Willow and Moreg shared a look.

'There's other things too,' continued Chopak. 'Well, my nephew, Raymar – he's been walking around in a daze for days; he was meant to be married – it's so bizarre, because we're just not sure if he actually *was*. All he keeps saying is he can't remember.'

'The trouble is, neither can we,' said Ybaer.

Moreg nodded. 'That makes sense – it matches what we've seen too.' And she explained to them about the missing day and her fear that it had been stolen.

Ybaer gasped. 'You believe it was taken away? And all the memories with it?'

'I'm afraid so,' said Moreg. 'But we are going to try to get it back.'

As Willow listened a giant purple hat with a long green feather swam before her eyes, her grandmother's face turned away from her, and she felt something inside her clench in icy cold fear, but just as quickly as the image appeared in her mind it was gone. She couldn't help wondering if all the others had forgotten something, something that had happened on Tuesday – had *she*?

Ybaer seemed to stare at Willow for a long moment as if considering her. Then she nodded. 'We can help you with *this*,' she said, snapping a small twig from a sapling that gleamed with a blue haze and handing it to Willow. 'This is a stealth sprig, it will help you to become invisible. As it has been taken from its source it will only work the once. Use it wisely when the time comes. You will know when that is.'

Willow blinked. 'You want me to have it?' she asked. 'Not . . . Moreg?'

The Mementon nodded. 'Only a child can use it.'

Willow looked at Moreg, who seemed unsurprised; in fact, she looked rather pleased – as if it were only natural that she'd been given a strange magical twig to help her become invisible. Willow stuttered her thanks and put the twig inside a small pocket inside her carpetbag,

sharing a puzzled look with Oswin as she did.

Ybaer smiled. 'Come, follow me – we'll get you matched to a broom.'

Willow blinked and a furl of sudden excitement sprang inside her.

They followed Ybaer and Chopak to a small wooden workshop where several of the new brooms were suspended above the floor of the workshop. He rubbed his beard while he eyed Moreg, a shrewd look on his face. Finally he nodded. 'Perhaps something modern . . . something that doesn't play around? It doesn't happen often, but, like I said, every now and then you get a broom that is open to a little bit of experimentation. A bit of modification.'

Eyes shining, he raced off to the back of the showroom, coming back with a monster of a broom, a wide grin spreading across his face.

Willow had never seen anything like it: it had a low-slung broom handle, spikes for footrests and on either side was an *engine*, which roared to life when Chopak pulled a cord from each. Bright orange flames shot out behind as the broom streaked off, doing a thunderous loop around them and making them all duck for safety. It came to a halt right in front of Moreg.

Chopak handed her a pair of flying goggles. 'I call it "The Business",' he said with a wide smile, which to all their shock Moreg returned. She ran a hand along its polished length, saying, 'Perfection! A broom, but *not* a broom.' Her eyes were alight.

There was a hushed silence. After some time he closed his mouth, then turned to Willow. 'Now, yours . . . I already know. As soon as I saw you I thought . . . this is the girl.'

He came forward with a mid-sized broom that glided as light as a feather. Its wood had a silvery sheen and mixed in with the twigs were long white tail feathers. It was simply beautiful. While she stared it seemed to disappear before their eyes, blending in with the surroundings.

'This,' said Chopak, leaving the broom to suspend next to Willow's hip, 'is Whisper. It's a very rare Stealth-Racer. This one is most unusual; we found it on Wednesday and no one remembers making it – which is odd as it has these unusual tail feathers. They remind me a little of a cloud dragon's feathers, but that's impossible, of course; cloud dragons have been gone from Starfell for years. Go on, give it a whirl.'

77

Heart pounding, Willow gripped the sleek handle, swung a leg over and sat astride. The broom hovered very slowly off the ground, but when she touched off with her toes it shot up faster than she could blink. She soared high, past the trees, her carpetbag clamped beneath her arm. Oswin's green eyes peered out as he gasped, *'Oh no!'*

78

She did a loop, then rejoined the others (and her stomach, which had plummeted to the ground). It was without a doubt the best moment of her life and she couldn't stop smiling.

But reality came crashing down hard as Willow mentally calculated her spurgles and knew she didn't have a hope in Starfell of being able to afford Whisper.

But when they asked the price Chopak insisted that the brooms were gifts. 'We want to aid your quest, so consider it our gift – our way of helping you to rediscover the missing day. Good luck, young Willow,' he said as she stuttered her thanks.

Despite their better intentions to press on with their journey, it was noon when they finally left Radditch. Not that Willow minded. She'd loved her time with the Mementons – and now, wonder of wonders, she was leaving on her very own broomstick.

The only one who seemed resolutely unimpressed was Oswin, who had found his voice now that they were far away from the Mementons. **'Go on a journey, she said,'** he muttered darkly. **'Save the world, she said,'** he harrumphed. **'She din't say *nuffink* about flying on no blooming brooms.'**

*On the edge of a forest, not very far away, a boy sat by the campfire planning his vengeance against the people*

who had tried to thwart him. His face was shrouded beneath his hood, his eyes dark as they stared at the flames. His fingers touched the box he had once been imprisoned for possessing.

He was anxious to have it be done with now. To stop with the pretence once and for all.

An old man clamped a hand on his shoulders. 'We will find them, son,' he said. 'And what a glorious triumph it will be.'

'Yes, Father,' said the boy, quickly stowing the box out of sight.

The man smiled indulgently, then turned back to the others. He longed to return to the fortress, to his comfortable bed . . . but the rumours that had reached them – that the witch would finally be breaking the law and might be seized were too good to miss. He picked up his flagon and joined the others in prayer.

He didn't see the way the boy's mouth twisted when he'd left. Or the look of revulsion that had marred his features at his father's touch. He hadn't seen how the boy's heart had turned to stone. If he had, he may have suspected what lay inside that dark heart, and how it vowed that the triumph would be his alone . . .

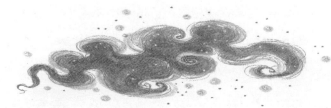

# 6

## The (Newly) Forbidden City of Beady Hill

One of Willow's happiest memories was when one of Granny Flossy's potion experiments went wrong and she ended up making chocolate instead. Willow thought that had been pretty near perfect happiness, until now. Flying Whisper past winding silvery lakes, and through the seemingly endless expanse of cloudless sky, all she could do was smile.

She was partly frozen, her hair had turned into one large knotty helmet that had bird droppings in it from a pigeon who'd used her as target practice, and Oswin hadn't taken a break from moaning, but she was utterly, blissfully happy.

Well, until a volley of flaming arrows streaked past her broom, almost causing her to fall in her fright. She screamed and clung on to Whisper.

'They're just warning arrows. Looks like the king's army has claimed the air space here . . . We'll have to land before the city's walls,' said Moreg, racing up to her side. 'They won't let us pass over. Better to go on foot, then we can fly on after we've found any clues to the forgotten teller's whereabouts.'

Heart stuttering in fear, Willow followed after Moreg, trying to keep clear of the orange flames that erupted from the Business's engines.

Willow's heart was still in her throat. Up on the ramparts she could see the archers with their flaming arrows.

They made way for the outer wall of the city, landing away from prying eyes. 'They're a bit sticky when it comes to magic around here,' explained Moreg, 'and being on a broomstick will just anger them further. Best to just blend in for now.'

Willow nodded. Though her heart was still racing.

'I'll pop the brooms into my pantry for safekeeping – it'll be better not to advertise who we are to the army.'

Willow agreed, though she kept a hold of the hairy carpetbag with Oswin inside.

As they headed towards the city's walls there was a

83

distinctive high-pitched panicking noise coming from the bag, which was slightly alarming. *'Oh **no**! Oh, me **greedy** aunt! Osbertrude, **why'd** yew **curse** us kobolds?'*

In Willow's experience Oswin only got this panicked when he detected powerful magic approaching and was feeling particularly afraid. Incidentally this happened every time her sister Camille was about to enter their bedroom.

But before she had a chance to worry about why he was reacting this way Moreg said 'Bother' in a resigned sort of way as a tall, skinny boy dressed in a long brown robe with three golden arrows emblazoned across the chest rounded the town wall and gaped at them in apparent surprise. He had very straight, almost straw-like blond hair, which looked like it had been thatched to his head, and his pale face was generously peppered with pimples. He made the sign of Wol by holding both hands together and pointing his second and last fingers up. Then, before they could stop him, he screamed, 'WITCHES!' This was followed closely by, 'BROTHERS! THEY ARE HERE!' and he hastened away, presumably to get the others.

'That was a Brother of Wol, right?' asked Willow

in dismay, watching him leave. The trouble with the Brothers of Wol was that if you found one, you were sure to find others; they were a bit like roaches.

Moreg nodded, pinched the bridge of her nose as if she had a headache and said, 'I was afraid of this – I had hoped we had more time.'

'Afraid of what?' asked Willow, eyes following in the direction the Brother of Wol had gone. 'Um, don't you think we should make a run for it?'

'Not yet, no.' Moreg pursed her lips and reached into the pocket of her dress, where she fished out a bronze disc about the size of a large flat biscuit. Peering over Moreg's elbow, Willow saw that it had a large brass needle and resembled a compass, although the destinations seemed more nonsensical than geographical. There was one that read '*Turning Point*', another that suggested '*Cup of Tea?*', one that said, '*If I Were You, I'd Run*', another that warned '*There be Dragons*', and one that appeared to commiserate with '*One Might Have Suspected as Such*'.

The needle was currently pointing to '*One Might Have Suspected as Such*'.

Moreg sighed resignedly. 'So that's that then.'

Willow frowned. 'What *is* that thing?'

'Oh, this?' Moreg said. 'It's a StoryPass; got it in the town of Library. Apparently it's meant to help with novel cataloguing, but I find it useful in life too. Here, take a look,' she said, handing it to Willow.

While Willow was looking at the strange compass-like object, a low, drawling voice from behind said, 'Well, well. If it isn't Moreg Vaine? This is a surprise – caught in the act of attempting to enter the forbidden city of Beady Hill, I see. *Tut-tut.*'

They turned to find a portly, bald Brother, whose small black pebble eyes were shining with glee. Next to him were several more Brothers of Wol, including the young one from earlier.

The portly Brother was dressed slightly differently to the others; his brown robe had a red circle in the middle, and the three golden arrows inside it were pointing up. Willow wondered if this marked him as some kind of senior Brother.

'Forbidden city?' asked Willow, looking at Moreg in surprise. Surely the witch hadn't knowingly brought them to one of the areas that outlawed entry to magical people?

'*Newly* forbidden,' admitted the Brother with the red circle. He allowed himself a small, sinister grin, which belied his next words. 'We are not monsters; we've allowed the former residents a week to gather their belongings . . . But, yes, forbidden *now* – you are trespassing on the first official day . . .'

Moreg's eyes glittered. 'Former residents – with nowhere to go now as a result? Kicked out of their homes because the only crime they have committed is to be different from you?'

The Brother sniffed. 'Well, if by different you mean

*dangerous*, then yes . . . different. It makes sense then to have them separated. We cannot let you leave, you see. I'm sure you can appreciate our predicament?'

'And mine,' said Moreg, her voice mild, but more ominous somehow. 'I am in the company of a child, after all, and I wouldn't want to see her threatened, you understand. I may very well have to react a bit . . . you see.'

'React a bit *what*?' The bald Brother frowned.

'A bit unfortunately towards you . . .'

The Brother paled slightly, his earlier bravado slipping somewhat. 'See here . . . there are consequences for breaking the law.'

'Indeed?' said Moreg.

'There are rules, that even you, Ms Vaine, cannot deny any longer,' he spat. 'I am the *High Master of the Brothers of Wol* . . . and you are under arrest, witch, for attempting to enter a forbidden area.'

'I understand,' said Moreg as the young Brother with spotty skin and blond hair came forward with two pairs of iron manacles that appeared to glow with an odd, almost *magical* light.

Willow frowned as she considered the manacles; they looked odd. Willow gasped as she realised. 'Those

manacles have been magicked!'

'Well, how else would you lock up a witch?' scoffed the High Master. Some of the Brothers next to him started chuckling.

From within the bag Oswin muttered darkly **''Tis a bit rich, don't** you **fink?** I mean, they **don'** want **magic** in the world, but **they** isn't afraid **to use** it?'

'Shhhhh,' whispered Willow, giving the carpetbag a shake, though she couldn't help but agree with him. She could hear Oswin grumble. **'Jes** sayin' . . .'

Moreg gave the High Master a thin smile. 'Fascinating. But you see there are rules for me as well. Rules that I too must follow. Rules about fairness, about freedom, against bullying . . . Rules in short that protect those in my charge.'

Above their heads thunder shook the sky, which turned instantly dark. The noise was deafening, and very close to where they were standing a bolt of lightning shot down and scorched the ground.

The High Master jumped. There were burn marks from the lightning on the ends of his robe. 'See here,' he said, gulping, his eyes wide, 'you *were* about to enter Beady Hill. I have *no* choice; I have to take you both.'

The witch stared at him for some time, her black eyes glittering in the sudden gloom. 'I think you'll find that even in the darkest, most hopeless of times there is always a choice when you look hard enough. Even if that choice is simply about how you will act. For instance, if I were you, I would choose to take only me. This is a choice, that I for one would have no cause to –' she waved a hand, and all of the Brothers flinched – 'make a fuss over.' There was a ghost of a smile about her lips.

The High Master cleared his throat. 'But I have to—'

Thunder ripped the sky once more, and a second bolt of lightning shot from above, leaving a fiery burn inches from the Brother's feet. He didn't jump, but his portly cheek flexed in anger, and he made a low, almost hissing sound.

'I beg your pardon?' said Moreg.

He looked at her. 'I suppose we can let the child go . . . with a warning.'

The other Brothers agreed.

Moreg nodded. 'I think that's best, yes.' Then, straightening up, she said, 'Very well,' and the darkening sky turned to dusk once more, and the

sound of thunder died instantly, as she stepped forward so that they could arrest her.

Had Willow looked down at the StoryPass in her hands she would not have been a bit surprised to see that the needle was currently indicating '*Turning Point*'. But she was far too busy staring at Moreg and the Brothers in horror.

'What? No!' exclaimed Willow.

The High Master stepped forward and quickly fastened the glowing manacles on to Moreg's wrists.

'Y-you can't let this happen!' Willow shouted.

The Brothers were clearly wary of Moreg, and she'd just turned the world dark and made thunder and lightning strike! How could *Moreg Vaine* – the most powerful witch in all of Starfell – allow herself to be captured?

Willow shook her head. 'I'll come with you – maybe we can break out? I doubt they could keep us there long . . .'

'No! I will be going – you will not,' said Moreg, her voice fierce, brooking no argument.

Moreg bent down and whispered into her ear. 'I'm sorry, I'd hoped we had more time. Find the Sometimes house in the Ditchwater district; it's one

of the oldest magical houses in the area. They have moved on now, as all oubliers do, but look for clues to where their son, Nolin, has gone.'

'How can you be sure?'

Moreg's eyes were hazy for a moment, then they focused on Willow, and she blinked. 'Trust me. Look for the house with the yellow door; find the strange garden . . . It'll lead you to him, I'm sure.'

'Now, witch!' called the High Master.

Moreg nodded. She looked at Willow and said, 'You can do this,' and she started to walk away, followed by the Brothers.

'Wait!' cried Willow, her heart thudding painfully in fear as she rushed after her. 'I can't do it without *you*!'

Moreg lifted a hand to pat Willow's shoulder, and one of the manacles popped off her wrists. 'You'll be fine.'

A Brother behind Moreg gasped. Moreg looked at him with what almost seemed like sympathy, shrugged, then popped the manacle back on where it remained unfastened. 'Never mind, I can just hold it in place.'

Willow's mouth fell open. 'They don't even *work* on you!' she gasped. 'Why are you going with them when you could fight this?'

'Sometimes you just have to do what's right,' said Moreg.

The High Master seemed to inflate with pride at this. 'Quite right.'

'But this is *wrong*! It's their stupid rules, not ours! We hadn't even entered Beady Hill yet, so it's not like we broke any rules! How can you just agree to this? How can I go on without *you*?'

'Don't worry; it's how it should be. Remember, Willow: *practical makes perfect.*' She looked up at the sky and nodded. 'And, when you think of it, a little rain is essential for uncovering what you might need.'

Willow looked up but there was no rain. Was this really the time for the witch to lose the plot?

Moreg looked at her. Her face was very serious and Willow thought for a moment that now the witch would say something wise, something that explained why she'd decided to abandon their mission and allow herself to be imprisoned by a bunch of crazy, fanatical priests, priests who Willow was sure the witch could fight off if she tried, despite their number – she had made lightning strike!

'The pantry,' said Moreg.

Willow's eyes popped in disbelief. 'The pantry?'

93

'Yes, whenever I feel truly lost I go there. There's something about it that just brings the answer to light. Perhaps it's the presence of food, which can be rather soothing. I daresay it may help you too in the end, if you give it a try.'

Willow blinked. The witch truly was mad. How on Starfell was that supposed to help her?

She whirled round, facing the High Master. 'Where are you taking her?' she demanded.

For a moment she thought he wouldn't answer, then he gave her an odd look as if it were obvious and chortled. His plump cheeks pink with pleasure at the idea of taking *Moreg Vaine* there. 'Wolkana, of course.'

Willow paled. The hidden monastery of Wolkana was a fortress, the stuff of legend. It was created thousands of years before to safeguard the Brothers from those with magic. People said it had been built by Wol himself so that a person with magic in their veins couldn't find it, even if they were standing directly across from it. How would she be able to save Moreg from there?

Willow watched in horror as the Brothers and Moreg walked on, growing smaller and smaller as they went past the gates and down the hill and out of sight.

Willow set the carpetbag down on the ground and fought the urge to scream. An hour ago she was on a mission to save the world with the most powerful witch in all of Starfell. Now the witch was gone, and she had no idea how to get into the forbidden city all by herself, and all she had with her was the monster from under the bed for company.

She didn't even have her new shiny broom, Whisper, as it was stowed away in the witch's portal pantry, which meant that if by some miracle she did find out where the forgotten teller was, and that seemed like a big if, it wasn't like the witch had a real plan, aside from looking for clues at an old house. He could be anywhere on Starfell . . .

She put her head in her hands and groaned. 'This isn't tricky, Moreg. It's *impossible*.'

Oswin stuck out his green furry head from the hairy carpetbag, blinking his orb-like eyes against the sudden daylight, and asked, **'Wot house was she going on about?'** Clearly he felt more confident when it was just the two of them. Though as a creature that liked the dark, he preferred to stay inside the carpetbag most of the time.

Willow sighed, then stood up. There was no point in falling apart; it wouldn't bring the witch back. 'The Sometimes house, apparently. The old family home of the forgotten teller.'

His shaggy green coat turned from lime to carrot instantly. **'An' it's in there – the city that yew was almost locked up fer entering?'** he said, pointing a fluffy paw at the granite-coloured wall.

'*Yes.*' Willow looked at the StoryPass, which was still in the palm of her hand, the needle pointing to '*One Might Have Suspected as Such*', and shook her head.

# 7

## Amora Spell

Willow picked up the carpetbag with a sigh. 'Maybe there is some gap in the city wall that is unguarded?' she muttered, her eyes scanning the perimeter.

As she inched closer she saw, however, that there were a lot of soldiers milling about overseeing the exodus of witches and wizards. Not to mention the guards keeping an eye out on the ramparts. It was impenetrable.

'This is bad.'

From within the bag she heard Oswin sympathise. **'I knows. She never even left you 'er cloak ... Wot we gonna nibble now, eh?'**

Willow rolled her eyes. She'd meant it was bad that they were doing checks. 'Thank you, Oswin.' Clearly the fact that Moreg had taken their access to food

with her was of far more consequence to the kobold than the real problem – that they somehow needed to get inside a heavily fortified city undetected.

As she sank deeper into despair Willow noticed a donkey cart piled high with clothing approach the entrance. It was driven by a portly man with an impressive handlebar moustache. He stopped a few feet in front of them, almost blocking their view.

The man was asked to show some form of identification, and she heard him say, 'Laundry service. The duke likes to have his delicates sent to Lael . . . You know what they say about elves and washing . . .'

'What?' asked the guard.

'Oh? Well, they're good at it . . .'

'I thought there was going to be a joke.'

'Why would you think that?'

'See, when you said it like that, "You know what they say about elves and washing," there's usually about to be some kind of a joke.'

'You calling elves funny or something?'

The two started to argue. The laundry man said something about elvish discrimination, and having a great-grandmother who was part elf.

Willow stopped listening as Oswin's green paw

came out of the bag and tapped her. '**If yew** really wants **to get inside, mebbe we could jes climb inside** that fing, **and hide** under that pile o' rags? **Jes saying.**'

He seemed to be looking at the scene from a small hole in the bag, so all Willow could see was one luminous green eye.

Willow stared at him, her mouth falling open in amazed delight.

'Wot?'

She peeked past the cart and inched closer. It was true – the guards *were* distracted by the laundry man, who was now having a hard time explaining why his papers had bite marks on them (from the donkey it seemed). So, while the men were occupied, Willow crept back behind the cart, and petted Oswin's green head in thanks. This was followed by a small purring sound and then swiftly by a cleared throat when she asked, 'Oswin, were you *purring*?'

There was a rather horrified hiss from inside the bag. '**Kobolds don' purr!**'

'But you just did.'

'**I is NOT a cat.**'

Smoke started curling from the top of the bag, and

Willow stifled a laugh. 'Sorry, my mistake.' Then she quickly picked up the bag, and slipped inside the cart, Oswin muttering darkly under his breath, '**I is the monster** from under **the bed . . .**' while she pulled a pile of clothing on top of them.

'Shhh,' she whispered, hoping that no one had seen them.

Finally they heard the laundry man say, 'Just so you know, the longer we stand here arguing, the more likely it is that the duke will think you were going through his unmentionables . . .'

Very shortly afterwards the cart's wheels were trundling inside the forbidden city of Beady Hill. Willow watched through a small gap in the piles of laundry as they passed by the guards, her heart in her throat.

When the cart had come to a stop sometime later, and the coast appeared to clear, she slid out, hairy carpetbag in hand. As she began to sneak away she heard, 'Oi, what you doing? You better not have taken any of the duke's delicates!' from the laundry man, and she broke into a run, snaking her way down a maze of cobbled streets.

When Willow's heart had finally slowed down, and she was sure that they were safe, she stopped and

took a proper look around. Hundreds of tall greyish houses, taller than they were wide, were hunched together as they snaked round the sloping hill, their glossy windows seeming to look down at her with a beady glint. And right at the top, surrounded by a dark, hazy cloud, she could just make out the grey stone ramparts where the archers were waiting.

She set the bag down as a group of people heading towards the market walked past. 'I wish I had a robe or something – something to help me blend in better.'

**'I fink that would jes makes yew stands out worse,'** observed Oswin from the hole in the bag.

Willow had to admit that he had a *point*, as most of the townspeople who passed them were dressed similarly to her. Some even worse. Just then an old man with more liver spots than hair hurried past her. He was wearing a very old and tatty cloak, and was carrying a threadbare, bulging knapsack. He was accompanied by an ageing grey cat, who looked more than a little defeated himself. 'Come on, Gurgle, we know when we aren't welcome.'

'Excuse me,' said Willow, approaching him slightly reluctantly, particularly when he shot her a very sour look. She cleared her throat. 'Um, sorry, would you

happen to know where I could find the Sometimes house? I was told they used to live in the Ditchwater district of Beady Hill.'

The man looked at her, then snorted, mumbling under his breath.

'Sorry?' said Willow.

He harrumphed again. 'Yes, well, *you* should be. The Sometimes family had the sense to move on years ago . . . Never thought this would happen in my city. First they told us we HAD to live here, and now they tell us we must get OUT? Don' even make sense. We've lived here for years peacefully, making the most of a bad situation, paying our taxes . . . contributin'. It's not like we deserved this; we've done nothing wrong,' he said, then walked off, shoulders slumped as if they carried the weight of the world.

Willow felt a pang of pity, realising that he must be one of the magical residents now forced to leave his home. 'He must have been a wizard,' she said.

'**Proberbelly a gizard**,' agreed Oswin as a group of girls walked past.

One of the girls had shiny blonde curls and was carrying a basket laden with iced buns. She gave Willow a look of surprise at her speaking aloud, apparently to herself. The look soon changed to one of disgust when she noticed Willow's hairy green carpetbag. The girl caught the eyes of her friends, and they erupted into whispers and giggles as they passed her. Willow picked up her bag, then followed the girls, though she really didn't want to after the way they'd laughed at her. 'Excuse me,' she said.

They turned to her in surprise, and the one with the blonde curls raised a pale eyebrow. 'I'm sorry, we're not interested in whatever you're selling.'

One of the other girls started giggling again. She stopped when Willow gave her A Look.

Willow took in a calm, steadying breath. She'd had a lot of practice what with having Camille for a sister. 'I'm not selling anything. I was just wondering if any of you know where I could find Ditchwater . . .'

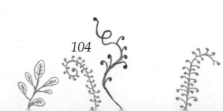

The blonde girl's face twisted with scorn. 'What do you want with that area? I heard they're going to start tearing it down . . . Not soon enough, if you ask me.'

Willow's frown darkened. 'Those are people's *homes*.'

The girl shrugged. 'Not any more. Didn't you hear about the new ruling? We've got Forbidden status now – no magical people allowed – which means that they've finally started kicking out the riff-raff.' Then she paused and smirked. 'Clearly they missed a few, though,' she said, eyeing Willow's dress with some disdain.

A girl with dark red hair, who hadn't giggled along with the others, reprimanded her. 'Kathleen!'

Willow closed her eyes for a second, then counted to three. She pushed down the top of Oswin's head as it began to rise out of the bag in outrage. She heard him mutter, **'I'll show 'er *riff-raff . . .*'**

'Can you point me towards it, please? It's important,' Willow said.

The girl with the red hair answered. 'If you follow this road, take a left by the river, and you'll find Ditchwater a bit further on. Er . . . be careful.'

'Thanks,' said Willow, giving the girl a grateful smile, then picked up the bag and made her way up the street, hearing the friends argue as she left. 'I don't

know what's got into you, Mabel. You've been acting odd for days. Ever since you took my dress last week.'

'I told you I *didn't* take it.'

'Then where is it? The last thing I remember was you trying it on last Monday night.'

Willow rounded the corner, and their voices died down. She could still hear Oswin's mutterings from the bag. **'Why'd yew push me down? I could 'ave taken 'er.'**

'Thank you, Oswin, I know – but I just want us to find what we need, and then get out of this city, without being noticed – and you, unfortunately, are very memorable.'

The kobold took this as a compliment and handed her an iced lemon bun that he'd stolen off the blonde girl. Willow grinned and took a small bite from a bit that wasn't covered in fur before handing it back.

The grey clouds above were threatening rain and the sun was low in the sky by the time she found the Ditchwater district, and Willow stopped in surprise. It was a floating village, which wound along the river. Some of the houseboats were a bit ramshackle and made of mismatched materials, but they were colourful, the

paint vibrantly hued in shades of pumpkin, sunshine and sapphire, as if the residents had tried their best to make this area as cheerful as they could. Suspended in the air by magic were lamps that still cast their amber lights on the water. Willow thought that this must be how the district got its name. She couldn't help thinking of her mother and Moreg growing up here.

As she walked along, past the houseboats, the path alongside the river widened and she could see that some of the older floating homes were slightly bigger, with portholes and wide decks with potted plants and garden furniture spilling over onto the banks. As she walked deeper into the district the houses became more traditional homes built on the ground, away from the water. Most of these, though, were now empty and boarded up. Ditchwater reminded Willow of a ghost town, one where even the ghosts had left in rather a hurry. Doors hung off hinges and many household items lay abandoned on the street as if the owner had decided it would be safer to run away than to go back and get them.

Just when Willow was wondering if all the residents had fled, a hag with long, greasy hair and a wart on her chin suddenly came tearing out of a stone

107

house that was covered with moss. She was loaded down with an assortment of household goods, which she put on to an already overloaded wheelbarrow nearby. She pulled at her long, straggly brown hair. 'The potions, can't forget the potions,' she muttered, then went racing back inside the house for the rest of her things, not even seeing Willow.

The hag had clearly heard about the new ruling and was making haste to pack up her things and get going before the Brothers of Wol came to take her away for trespassing inside the newly forbidden district.

Willow set her carpetbag down with a frown. There was something about the hag; she seemed almost familiar somehow. And she'd mentioned potions . . . There weren't that many potion-makers in Starfell . . . very few had the ability. She peered closer at the wheelbarrow, curious.

'**Wot** yew **doing?**' asked Oswin.

'I don't know. I might be wrong, but that might have been my granny's old potions partner,' she said, looking from the wheelbarrow to the house where the hag had gone. 'I met her once, I think, when I was little. It looked a bit like her . . . Granny used to say that if there was trouble . . . Amora Spell was not far behind.'

She turned back to the wheelbarrow, her nose wrinkling at the sight of curly rats' tails and jars full of what looked like eyeballs, rusty nails and toenail clippings. She picked up a jar and put it back with a shudder. These ingredients looked nothing like the sorts of things Granny Flossy used . . .

Suddenly Oswin's mutterings turned into high-pitched wails from within the hairy bag. **'*Oh no, oh no! Oh*, me horrid aunt! A *curse* upon *you*, Osbertrude, *from* all of us kobolds!'**

The hairs on Willow's body began to stand on end. She snatched her hand away from the wheelbarrow, then closed her eyes in mortification as a high-pitched voice asked, 'Can I help you, dearie?'

Willow straightened with a gulp. She turned to find the hag behind her, peering at her with wide black eyes, and Willow thought that staring into them was like looking inside a long empty well. Oswin wasn't the only one whose knees started knocking.

'Or you just interested in stealing things that don' belong to you?' she hissed.

Willow's eyes popped. 'I – no – I was just looking . . .'

The hag's eyes darkened. 'Thought you'd help yerself, that it?'

109

Willow shook her head fast.

A faint scent of smoke began to curl from out of the carpetbag.

The hag sniffed. Then seemed to consider Willow, head cocked to the side. 'Is it a potion that yer after, eh? A love potion, dearie?' she asked, waggling a set of shaggy eyebrows that turned up at the corners. She gave her a gummy, toothless leer, transforming instantly into the picture of friendliness at the idea of a sale.

Willow shook her head and the hag frowned, her smile fading. Something that Granny Flossy said floated in Willow's mind. *'The only potion-maker daft enough to meddle with matters of the heart was old Amora Spell, though the only thing she's ever managed to give anybody was heartburn. Heh-heh-heh . . .'*

'You're Amora Spell, aren't you?' asked Willow.

The hag eyed her suspiciously. 'Who's asking?'

'I think you used to know my granny . . . You came past the house once when I was little . . . after she had the accident.'

'Oh?' said the hag, straightening slightly, her ink-coloured eyes raking over Willow with suspicion. 'And who is yer *granny*?'

'Florence Moss.'

As she said her grandmother's name aloud a part of Willow's mind waited, as if it were about to remember something important, but a larger, stronger part of her mind shut down quickly, as if it were a suitcase and someone had sat on it to keep it closed. She tried to hold on to the wisp of thought that had appeared, blue-tinged and plunged in sadness, but it was like holding on to the wind. She blinked, and all too soon it was gone, punctured by the sound of the hag's wild cackling laughter.

'Caw-caw-caw, ghn-ghn. Flossy Mossy?' She chortled as tears ran down her long nose while she slapped a knee in apparent glee.

Willow managed to give her a haughty stare, which only made the hag laugh harder still. When at last she had composed herself with much 'Ghn-ghn, oh my goodness, caw-caw-caw!' She took a deep, rattling sort of breath, which exposed blackened stubs for teeth, and asked, 'You one of Flossy Mossy's grandbabies? She still as mad as a cackling crow then?'

'She's not mad . . . Well, not completely,' protested Willow. Granny couldn't exactly help it; she just got confused sometimes.

This only made the hag laugh harder still.

At Willow's dark scowl Amora Spell wiped the

tears from her eyes. 'So which one is you then? Which grandbaby?'

News of her sisters had evidently spread. It was hard not to when one sister blew things up with her mind and the other used hers to move things. So, with all the confidence she didn't feel Willow declared, 'I'm the one you've heard all about.'

The hag looked at her for some time, and then very slowly she started to grin. 'Yes-s-s,' she said, inching closer, looking at Willow's hair, her eyes. Suddenly a claw-like hand snaked tightly round Willow's arm. 'That's what I was thinking meself . . . Coming 'ere, going through my things . . . Speaking about me old potions partner . . . I suppose she blamed me for that explosion, didn' she . . . when it was her own daft fault.'

Willow frowned. 'She said it was an *accident*.'

'Yes, that's right, it was an accident. That's what I tol' her . . . She had no right to question me the way she did . . .'

'Question you? Why did she question you? Did you have something to do with it?'

'*What did you just say?*' hissed the hag. 'Are you accusing me o' something? I don' appreciate that, not one bit.'

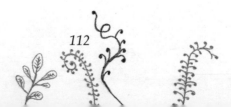

112

The StoryPass Willow was still holding was suggesting, *'If I Were You, I'd Run'*.

Amora sniffed. 'I know exactly which grandbaby *you* are. You is the one that stays home to look after the old croat now that she's gone banana doolally. The one whose magic is a bit, well, humdrum, ain't cha? Finding people's lost bits and bobs – it's not really impressive now, is it?'

Willow wrenched her arm out of the old woman's grip, rubbing the skin. 'Well, that depends,' she said.

'On what?' asked the hag.

'On what I find,' said Willow, closing her eyes and raising a hand to the sky. Suddenly there was a flash of light and a dripping-wet fisher's net, twice as big as Willow, appeared in her outstretched palm.

'Ha!' sniggered the hag, slapping a skinny knee. ''Tis you! What you gonna do with that, girl?' she scoffed. 'Ketch yerself my lost socks? Frighten my nostrils to death?' She threw back her head and guffawed. She took a potion from out of her robe and uncorked it. The liquid inside began to glow a dark, oozing sort of blood red and her hand snaked forward towards Willow's mouth. 'I think maybe I need to teach you a lesson about what happens to little girls

who go around accusing people . . .'

Willow shut her eyes and held the fisher's net up to the sky, and suddenly a wave of green briny water cascaded from the heavens, and a colossal hairy fish with a set of razor-sharp, needle-like teeth landed with a whoosh into the net and began flopping around wildly, drenching them all.

The hag jumped back, all traces of humour fading fast. A bit of spilled potion hit the ground and began to smoke in a dark red puff.

'This is the Buzzle Wuzzle,' said Willow as the thing inside the net thrashed around madly.

'He's a lost lake monster
and he looks like he might like
to teach you a lesson himself!' she said,
flinging him at the hag, who screamed as it
flew at her with all its needle-like teeth bared.

Amora fell backwards over the wheelbarrow,
fighting off the fish, and in the kerfuffle Willow
picked up the carpetbag with Oswin still inside and
followed the StoryPass's advice by making
a run for it.

# 8

## The Sometimes House

Willow slowed down only once she was safely away on a long winding road deeper inside the district of Ditchwater.

'Horrid old crook,' she said, gasping for air, a hand on her knees. 'You – know –' she said, sucking in big draughts of air – 'Granny used to be the best potion-maker in all of Starfell before that accident . . .' She thought it was weird the way that Amora had seemed so cagey about it . . . Was it possible that she had something to do with it?

**'Was that before her hair turned green?'** asked Oswin from within the bag as Willow carried on, walking past streets that widened into avenues with small front gardens that spread into bigger lawns. This must be the oldest and wealthiest part of the suburb, she realised.

'I think so,' said Willow, who stopped to peer at some of the front gardens. Here and there the houses had names and plaques. But she couldn't see any yellow door and none of the gardens looked unusual, just overgrown and a bit wild really.

Suddenly something bright caught the corner of her eye. She turned and looked, but couldn't see anything. Then as she began to walk on by she passed a thin, long bridleway wedged between two houses and saw, at the end of it, something bright and yellow in the twilight. It was a door.

She stopped. 'Do you think this is it?' she whispered, peering up ahead at the long sweeping path, where very far in the distance she could make out what looked almost like a house.

**'Mebbe,'** said Oswin.

She looked at the StoryPass, which right then didn't seem to be offering much help, as it was currently suggesting, '*Cup of Tea?*'

They set off up the dark, overgrown path, Willow looking over her shoulder in case anyone was watching. She didn't want another run-in with Amora Spell, that was for sure. But they saw no one.

As they drew closer it became clear that the house

117

was old and dilapidated. It had chipped blue paint and a yellow front door. The garden was wild and covered in brambles. As she neared she saw dozens of colourful teapots fixed beneath the windows like curious flowerpots, with trailing plants spilling out of them.

'This must be it,' she breathed. She tried the door, which was locked, then walked round the back of the house, going past an assortment of old, discarded furniture. It looked like no one had been here for years.

The back door was off its hinges, and after a bit of struggling she managed to wedge it open.

Inside the house smelt of damp and neglect. It was getting dark but she could just make out signs of what had once been a family home – an old mustard-coloured sofa with a broken leg in one corner, which birds had used as a nest. On the walls she saw portraits of little old women and men all with white hair, and a young boy smiling while holding up a plant. She stopped to peer at it closely. *Now that is unusual*, she thought. The plant had funny blinking eyes. Was this who Moreg was referring to . . .? She walked down the passage, stepping over discarded bits of crockery and brushing against dusty curtains and disintegrating furniture. Whoever had lived here seemed to have left many years before . . .

She peered into a bedroom, which looked like it had belonged to the boy's parents. There was nothing in it besides an old, sagging bed and an empty wardrobe. She left and went through the last door, then stopped. For just a second she thought she had left the house, and walked into a garden. But on closer inspection she realised it was another bedroom, though it was filled with dozens of large pots containing curious plants, which sadly seemed mostly dead now. Their spots and fur had faded, the

strange-coloured leaves shrivelled. One of the walls was covered from floor to ceiling in pictures and sketches of even more plants. Wherever she stepped, her foot crunched dried leaves, feathers and flowers, and in the corner, the only nod to it being a bedroom at all really, was a single wooden bed.

She crept closer to the wall covered with pictures. They showed unusual-looking flowers and plants of all colours, shapes and sizes, with messy handwritten notes in the margins. Such as a hairy yellow plant with what looked like bushy eyebrows over odd cat-like eyes. A note next to it read, '*Likes shade. Feeds on old spiders.*' There were blue and gold ones, which according to the notes sang lullabies that put children to sleep. Others were translucent and looked like they had been dipped in watercolour paint. And on each sketch at the bottom was a note about where the plant was from.

It was a collection, she realised. Whoever drew these was interested in the most extraordinary, perhaps even the most magical plants.

The biggest drawing, however, was in the centre of the wall. It was of an enormous pale blue tree. Each branch had different-coloured blooms.

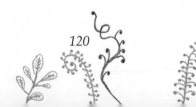

*

*Suddenly she was nine years old again, hiding away in the attic, hiccoughing as she cried big angry sobs, because her mother had said that she couldn't go with her sisters to the Travelling Fortune Fair.*

*'She doesn't love me like she loves them, that's what it is,' she told Granny Flossy, who had followed her up the stairs and had taken a seat next to Willow on an old bench.*

*'Nonsense,' said Granny. 'She loves you very much.'*

*'Then why can't I go?'*

*'Because yer too young, child. Those fairs aren't what you think they are – dark places some of 'em. Creepy, trust me. 'Tis no place fer a child.'*

*'Juniper went at my age.'*

*'Juniper is different; she can take care of herself.'*

*This was true. She could blow things up. Not like Willow.*

'It's because I don't have a power like hers. She's embarrassed of me . . .'

'No, I don't think it's that exactly. I think she's afraid that if yer not here, I'll blow the house up again.'

Willow snorted and couldn't help a small smile from forming. There was that. Though to be fair to Granny Flossy it hadn't been the whole house. Just a big part of the roof. And the spare room. And there was that time that she smashed all the windows in the greenhouse.

'Tell yer what – why don' I make us something special? Something you can't get at any fair?'

Willow sniffed. 'Like what?'

'Like maybe . . .' She peered into her hairy old green carpetbag, tapping her chin, her lime-green hair swinging in front of her face. 'Eternal youth?'

'So that I can never go to the fair?' scoffed Willow. 'That won't exactly help me, Granny.'

'Right, right, that one's tricky anyhow . . . Last time it went a bit wrong.'

Willow raised a brow. It had gone very wrong actually. To be honest most of Granny's potions went more than a bit wrong. There was the time when

Mrs Crone-Barrow developed that beard . . . which kept growing back no matter how much she shaved.

'Ah!' said Granny. 'I know, we'll make The Perfect Sunday Afternoon,' she said, pulling out a big glass jar full of strange green-and-gold pie-shaped blooms. She opened the jar and the scent that wafted over to Willow smelt sweet and delicious.

'What's that?'

'These are apple-pie blossoms – they're a key ingredient.'

'Apple-pie *blossoms*?' exclaimed Willow. She'd never heard of such a thing.

'Oh yes. You get all sorts of strange things growing in the magical forest of Wisperia. Even the trees are different colours . . . You know, they say that's where the magic hid when the Brothers of Wol tried to rip it away during the Long War . . . Anyway, it's the only place these flowers grow, on the Great Wisperia Tree itself. You can't miss it – it's the biggest of the lot and it's a really strange pale sort of blue. Never seen anything like it. It grows all sorts of things . . . but keep that between ourselves, right? Can't have everyone knowing my secrets . . . and where to get the best plants and ingredients . . .'

123

*The potion hadn't really worked. It had caused Willow to skip and sing for days, but they'd had a pretty good Sunday anyway.*

'Wisperia,' breathed Willow now. The largest, most magical forest in Starfell. Of course. It made sense. Few – apart from mad people like her granny – ever dared to venture there. It was an unpredictable place with magic fizzing about – they'd all heard the stories of people who'd come back changed as a result. Hooves for feet, hair that turned to flames, leaves for fingers . . .

It was supposed to be beautiful, and colourful, but it could be dangerous too – especially if you didn't know what you were looking for. It sounded like the perfect place someone who didn't want to be found would hide . . .

She stared at the picture of the tree, and then looked at the others, noting that most of them had the same handwritten note at the bottom. 'Wisperia,' she breathed again, touching one of the pictures. 'I think that's where he's gone . . . and where we'll have to head to next.'

There was faint gasp from the bag. **'Oh no.'**

# 9

## The Dragon's Tale

'I jes don' wanna go **back** to the Cloud Mountains. Yew **don'** understand . . . 'Tis not right . . . all these **big rocks** dangling in the sky **wiff nuffink** around them . . . 'Tis **creepy** and yer eyeballs don' works . . . I **means,** I like the dark . . . but I like the dark whens you can't **also falls off** . . .'

'The Cloud Mountains?' asked Willow, looking at him with a frown. 'But – that's not where we're going.' She stopped, then grinned, taking out the StoryPass, which just then pointed to *'One Might Have Suspected as Such'*. Oswin turned from green to orange, clearly a bit angry at himself as it dawned on him at the same time as Willow said, 'Oh – because that's the way to Wisperia, isn't it?'

In answer he put a paw over his eyes, then zipped the bag shut again. Willow could hear Oswin softly cursing his bad luck, and his *big mouth*, in High Dwarf. As well as something about being a cumberworld, whatever that was.

But, as much as Willow wanted to press ahead on their journey, she felt the exhaustion that had been creeping in after their long day start to take hold. She found herself struggling to keep her eyes open, and suggested they stop for the night. Oswin's sigh of relief was the last thing she heard before she fell fast asleep, curled round the hairy carpetbag on the small wooden bed, the air smelling faintly of flowers.

The next day, when Beady Hill was far behind them, Willow and Oswin passed a sign that read,

Cloud Mountains THIS WAY→
But I'd turn BACK if I were
YOU

A little further on one read:

Really, You can
Still TURN BACK

But the last one was probably the most ominous as it sort of gave up:

WE DID WARN YOU, stupid

Willow took a steadying breath as she went past it.

Fog was beginning to sweep the ground, and the air was cold as it slithered inside Willow's cloak, making the hairs on her neck stand on end. She shivered, though she wasn't sure if it was just the sudden chill. It had grown dark and grey, and she could no longer see her feet as she walked. She could make out odd shapes in the mist; as she neared one she found that it was a large rock, which looked a bit like a child. She swallowed, grabbing her chest when it seemed for a moment to look at her. Clutching the hairy carpetbag tightly, she walked past the rock-child fast, and saw through the swirling mist that they had rounded upon a mountain range that was suspended among the clouds so that it appeared to float in the air. *These must be the Cloud Mountains,* thought Willow. As she got closer the air grew even thicker with hazy mist and the familiar sound of Oswin's panicked wailing.

'OH NO! Oh no! Oh, me greedy aunt!

Osbertrude, a curse upon yeh. A curse, I tell yeh! I'm gonna die with only fruit in my bellllly . . .'

Willow felt her fear grow. His wails were reaching a deafening crescendo. He'd never been this panicked before, she thought. Not even when the Brothers of Wol or Amora Spell had appeared.

'What is it?' she asked, narrowing her eyes against the fog, trying to see.

Oswin shivered violently and zipped himself more securely into the hairy green bag.

Willow drew the StoryPass out of her pocket and went pale. 'Oh dear. It says *There be Dragons*,' she whispered. Her knees started to knock together. A faint '**eep**' came from Oswin's direction.

Then out of the swirling mist a voice like the wind howling on a cold night corrected her. '*Dragon.*'

'P-pardon?' stammered Willow, who took a step forward in spite of her knees, her eyes straining against the swirling mist.

'Just the *one* dragon,' said the voice, whistling in her ears. It sounded a little sad.

Willow felt something soft trail close to her face and she swallowed nervously. One dragon was *plenty*. The shaking bag in her hand told her that

Oswin wholeheartedly agreed.

'I – I didn't know there were still dragons in Starfell,' said Willow, thinking that perhaps if she kept talking he may decide *not* to eat them.

'There aren't many; just me and—' said the voice, which broke slightly.

'And who?' asked Willow, stepping closer.

In the haze she could just make out the ENORMOUS shape of the dragon, like a small mountain himself. He was covered in indigo-blue feathers that seemed to glow with an iridescent, pearly sheen; even his barb-like tail was covered in wispy dark-blue feathers. He was curled round a very large silver-gold egg about the size of Oswin. As she neared he turned his massive head and pinned her to the spot with a sad golden eye.

'A human child,' he said with what looked almost like a smile. There were certainly a lot of very sharp, glistening white teeth.

Willow swallowed, managing a nod.

The dragon looked at her. 'What is your name?'

'W-Willow.'

'I am called Feathering. For many years I was the last cloud dragon . . . until I found Thundera – my mate,' he said. A large sapphire tear formed at the

129

corner of his eye and landed on the egg. 'But she's left me now,' he said, slumping his head on top of the egg in a rather despondent way.

'Why did she leave you?' asked Willow, who couldn't help feeling a little sorry for the dragon.

'I was meant to be looking after the egg,' he said, tapping it very softly with a sharp jewel-like claw. His voice sounded like a mournful wail from a broken pipe.

'It was meant to hatch last week, you see. Thundera went hunting so that we would have enough food for when it arrived . . . but it never did.'

Willow gasped. 'What happened?'

'I don't remember!' he cried, lifting his head off the egg. 'I keep trying to – but I can't. I can't remember anything that happened that day. When I told Thundera that she became so angry she burnt down the whole side of the mountain,' he said mournfully. 'And, look, the egg – it's empty; though I don't know how that could have happened. It wasn't empty before, and I don't remember it hatching,' he said. Another tear slipped down his snout, landing with a heavy splash on Willow's foot, drenching it completely.

Willow felt desperately sad. She looked at the egg he was still cradling and her eyes began to smart. She inched forward and laid a hand on the tip of his wing.

'Was this last Tuesday?' she asked.

His golden eye slowly blinked. 'How did you know?'

In Willow's mind a giant purple hat with a long green feather swam before her eyes, her grandmother's face turned away from her, and she felt something hard and painful twist inside her belly. There was

something there, trying to get her attention. She bit her lip and shook the image away. 'Someone has stolen it, I think . . .'

'Stolen what?' he asked.

'The day.'

He lifted his head off the ground. 'Someone stole the day? But how? Who? Who would have done that?'

She shook her head. 'I don't know – but that's what I'm trying to find out. It's not just you – no one can remember what happened last Tuesday. All our memories of it are gone. It's like they've been taken . . .' She thought about it and said, 'But it's more than that – it's not just the memories; it's everything really.'

'What do you mean?'

Willow looked at the egg. 'It's worse than I imagined . . .'

And it was. It was all the births, the deaths, the weddings, the funerals, the arguments, the big things, the small things, all those incredibly special and mundane moments that go into the recipe of one ordinary day, making it something else, something quite extraordinary when you stop and really think about it as Willow did just then. She suddenly saw the

incredible value and significance of one ordinary day. Not just what happens on a single day, but how that day informs the next, giving it meaning and structure, and now what it meant to have it simply gone . . .

Her lungs forgot to breathe as she realised something. What wasn't she remembering? And why was it that every time she tried she saw Granny Flossy's hat? What did it mean?

The dragon lifted his large head, hope flickering in his eye. 'If it's been taken, can we get it back?'

'I don't know, but I'm going to try to find it.'

The dragon looked at her, taking in her small size, the state of her old, worn, rather uneven dress, the fisher's net in her rope belt and the green hairy carpetbag at her heels. 'You?' he asked. There couldn't have been a less likely candidate for saving the day than Willow Moss.

She shrugged. 'Yes. I have to try – I'm the only one who knows about it, and can do something about it, you see.'

The dragon looked at her for some time. Finally he said, 'You're not the only one who knows.'

'Sorry?'

'You're not the only one who knows it's missing –

not any more. You've told me and I'd like to help, if you'll have me.'

Willow blinked. 'You would help me?'

Feathering's claw tapped the egg very gently. 'If you're right – then maybe things will turn out differently.'

Willow nodded. 'They might.'

The dragon slowly started to sit up and the mountain around them started to rumble and shake from the movement. Willow found herself staggering backwards, the ground beneath her feet unsteady.

'What do we need to do?' asked the dragon.

'Do you know how to get to Wisperia?' she asked.

'I do.'

'Can you take me?'

'I can – if you carry this, please,' he said, handing over the egg. It was about as large as Oswin, who wasn't impressed when she opened the carpetbag and put it inside. One eye poked out of the top, turning from green to pumpkin, then back to green again as it took in the enormous size of Feathering. He gave a sheepish smile, then held out his arms and took the egg, giving it a gentle pat and a slight polish, then rather quickly he zipped the bag shut from the inside.

When Feathering looked from the bag to Willow in surprise she said, 'Don't ask.'

He nodded and bent down so that she could climb up on to his back, putting her legs behind his wing joints. She put the carpetbag between her knees and her arms round the dragon's neck, though they didn't reach very far.

'Hold on tight,' said the dragon.

From within the bag she heard a familiar **'Oh no! Oh, *me* horrid *aunt!*'** as Feathering took a few running steps that shook the mountain, causing an avalanche below, and launched himself into the air.

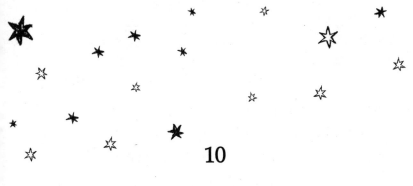

# 10

## The Forgotten Teller

As they whooshed up, up and up into the sky Oswin's panicked cries of *'Oh noooo! Oh, me greedy aunt! Where's me stove? Oh, Osbertrude!'* filled the air.

A part of Willow's mind was going *Oh nooooo* herself. It was one thing being on Whisper, and quite another being on a very large dragon, who flew over vast mountain ranges and wide sweeping rivers faster than she could blink. In fact, it was some time before she was able to open her eyes. When she did she gasped, though this time it had nothing to do with fear. The wind was icy and cold, but the view was spectacular; she could see the floating Cloud Mountains and, in the distance, a large colourful forest.

Wisperia.

It was unlike anything she'd ever seen before. In

the woods near her home in Grinfog the trees were all roughly the same – green leaves, brown bark and the occasional pretty flower. But this was something else entirely. The leaves were in shades of electric blue, sunset pink, violent orange and bright magenta. It looked like someone had upended a paint box over the horizon. She couldn't believe what she was seeing. It was like the pictures in the forgotten teller's room brought to life.

'You okay there?' came Feathering's voice.

'Y-e-s-s,' said Willow, feeling vaguely frostbitten as they flew through cloud. She was realising that flying on the back of a dragon was just as good as flying on a broomstick!

She lifted her arm to the sky, and a few seconds later her grandmother's old, rather hideously lumpy green-and-brown quilt came hurtling through the sky. Willow wrapped it round herself gratefully.

Though she knew later she'd have to 'lose' it again, she was glad of its warmth.

'**If you was back home, you'd be doing the washing now,**' observed Oswin, his one eye peeking out of the top zipper and staring out into the distance with a scowl, his fur the colour of pea soup. He swallowed, looking rather sickly.

She grinned widely. 'I *know.*'

'**I likes washday,**' he grumbled. '**You leaves me to sleep usually – and don' put me in a smelly bag made o' hair and go flyings with blooming great feathered beasts.**' He groaned, then zipped himself back inside.

Feathering ignored Oswin's grumblings. 'Where to in Wisperia?' he asked in his deep, wind-rattling-a-doorknob voice.

'I guess we could start by finding the tree.'

'In a forest?' It sounded like the dragon was laughing. There was a tinkling sound like a wind chime.

'I think it'll be blue and really big.' As she stared she saw that there were trees of all different colours. 'This is mad,' she said with a sigh, wondering how they'd find it with so many strange-coloured trees around.

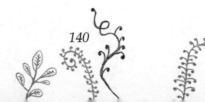

As they got closer to the forest, though, Feathering breathed. 'Maybe not so mad. Look,' he said, tilting his head to the left.

Willow stared. An enormous tree dominated the entire forest. It was the colour of blue sea glass and was about as wide as several farmhouses stuck together. It reached out to the very top of the sky, and was shrouded in bright white swirling clouds. Perched at the very top of the tree was a small wooden house, surrounded entirely by clouds. It looked as if it were floating on air, but she could just make out the stilts creaking softly as it swayed slightly in the wind. As they drew closer Willow saw teapots strung below the windows filled with an array of plants, just like those they'd seen in Ditchwater.

'That must be the forgotten teller's house!' she exclaimed, pointing.

Feathering nodded and flew towards the very top of the enormous tree. He landed on a branch the size of a large road, causing the tree to shudder and shake.

Willow slipped off Feathering's back, her knees wobbling as she did and her hands firmly clutching her carpetbag.

Feathering inclined his massive blue head. 'Who's choosing a slightly *extreme* way to get out of having a bit of company. Look!'

While Willow did think calling a large dragon a *bit* of company seemed a stretch, she saw that he was right. A tall spindly man wearing lots of lumpy clothing with odd bits of vegetation poking out of every pocket was currently fleeing the house with everything he could carry, including a tea set and a large brown dog, with a tongue the length of a soup ladle, squashed beneath his armpit. Only the man was running the wrong way and he almost slammed straight into Willow before he looked up.

'Gadzooks!' he exclaimed, rocking backwards on his heels, and dropping the teapot, which slopped tea everywhere. He had enormous pale blue eyes and long, wispy all-white hair, which made him look like an old man, even though he was probably quite a bit younger than her father. It was the boy from the portrait, she realised, the one with the plant that had all those blinking eyes. Except now he was grown up.

'Um – sorry?' tried Willow, though it was hardly her fault that he had almost run into her . . .

The man took an involuntarily step backwards as if she might bite. His mouth opened but didn't close. Willow saw that he was wearing what looked like every bit of clothing he possessed, including a necktie shaped like a bird in flight. He also seemed to have more pockets than his skinny frame should allow – all of which were bulging, some overflowing with bits of vegetation and others that seemed to be regarding them with interest.

Willow could have sworn that a leafy tendril waved at her.

Just then the man smacked his forehead, his eyes going from blue to white and back again in an instant, and Willow wondered if she'd imagined it when he started to laugh, his thin shoulders shaking. 'My old room . . . the pictures . . . You figured it out,' he said with an admiring sort of laugh, and Willow wondered if he'd seen it as a vision or simply guessed. His smile faltered fast, though, when he looked past Willow and finally seemed to spot Feathering. His face went the colour of ash, his eyes seemed to pop, and he silently mouthed the word 'dragon' before he keeled over backwards in a dead faint.

'Oh bother,' said Willow.

She took the StoryPass out of her pocket, which commiserated with '*One Might Have Suspected as Such*'.

'Happens all the time,' said Feathering, shrugging a colossal blue wing. 'Humans always faint when they see us now – it's like they think a cloud dragon would actually *eat* a human. Can you imagine?' he said in apparent disgust.

'Er,' said Willow, who was not about to admit that

that had been precisely her first thought when she'd first encountered him.

'*I* **din't** faint,' said a voice from within the hairy carpetbag.

Feathering looked at the bag and said, 'I don't think we've formally been introduced.'

The bag started to shake and there was a faint '*oh no*' sound.

'That's Oswin,' she said. 'He's a little shy . . .'

There was a low gasp. Then a furry tangerine head with pointed ears shot out of the bag, pumpkin-coloured eyes blazing in fury. '**I isn't** *shy*! **I is a little scared** of **that great** feathery beast,' he said, pointing with a long rusty claw. '**'E don' eat humans, so** 'e says. **'E never said nuffink** about *not* **eating** kobolds – but that don' mean **I's** *shy*,' he huffed, crossing his paws. Then he shot back inside the bag fast.

Apparently there could be nothing worse than being a *shy* monster.

'My apologies,' said Feathering, who looked like he was struggling not to laugh.

A noise came from the floor. The forgotten teller's eyes were open wide, yet they'd gone a strange, almost

filmy white. Willow waved a hand in front of his face but there was no response. A second later, she startled when a loud bark of laughter erupted from his motionless form, which was rather disconcerting as his eyes were still white. A second later his eyes turned blue again and he said, 'The Buzzle Wuzzle? On her head?'

He sat up, dislodging the dog, who was still tucked under his arm, but who had managed to go to sleep.

Willow stared. Had he just seen her memories?

He suddenly stopped laughing, his gaze falling on Feathering, his large blue eyes growing very sad. 'It just never hatched?'

Feathering nodded, his golden eye downcast.

The figure's eyes filled. 'Well, that's – I'm so sorry.' He blinked, his eyes went pale once more and he was out for the count again.

'This can't be good for him,' Willow observed.

**'How 'as 'e not fallen off this tree?'** asked Oswin.

Willow could just make out one now green eye, observing the proceedings from the hole in the hairy carpetbag.

'Good question,' said Feathering.

'Tuesday? Gadzooks!' said the prone figure, his eyes still opaque.

146

*The Forgotten Teller*

'Do you think he's unwell?' asked Willow.

**'Barking,'** muttered Oswin.

A loud snore erupted from the prone figure, followed by a snort from the dog, who opened a bleary eye, then rolled over and tried to go back to sleep. Then, suddenly, the man sat up again, carrying on the conversation as if he hadn't just fainted several times in under five minutes.

'Tuesday has gone missing!?' he cried.

'How did you know?'

'I saw your memory. That's what I do – I see the past.'

Willow nodded. Moreg had explained that. But she never said anything about how hazardous it seemed for him. 'Is that how come you fainted? We weren't sure if you were unwell or not.'

He stood up, thoroughly affronted, and made an attempt to brush himself off, which left lots of vegetation everywhere, making him look even more dishevelled. 'I have never fainted a day in my life!'

Willow blinked. 'Er – but—'

'You just did,' pointed out Feathering.

**'Least free times,'** confirmed Oswin. **'Choo'd fink 'e'd live someplace else besides the top of a tree, if 'e was in the 'abit o' fainting,'** he observed.

'I do *not* faint.'

'O-kay,' said Willow, sharing an incredulous look with Feathering and Oswin's shocked, now tangerine eye.

'I have visions . . .' said the forgotten teller, while he waved a hand in the air, only he'd picked up the teapot again, so cold tea went flying everywhere. 'Oh,' he said, putting the teapot down. 'The visions cause me to temporarily disconnect from the present . . . I suppose it *seems* like fainting but it's entirely different . . .'

'Oh **"vijuns"**, so different, **yes,**' huffed Oswin.

'Oswin,' said the figure, 'a kobold – that's what you're telling people?'

Oswin cleared his throat. '**On me mother's side . . .**'

'But your father— I mean, *well*—'

'**I is NOT a cat!**' harrumphed Oswin. Smoke started to curl out of the top of the bag. This was followed by some wild rambling. '**Peoples 'aving no respect for monsters nowadays. I is the monster from under the bed.**' He sniffed.

The forgotten teller smiled. 'I am Nolin Sometimes,' he said. 'Pleased to meet you, Willow, Feathering and Oswin.'

Willow's mouth fell open. 'You know our names – wow!'

He shrugged. 'Part of telling the past. This is Harold,' he said, indicating the sleeping dog.

'He's sweet,' said Willow, eyeing the fluffy creature.

From within the bag there was a harrumph sound. They all stared at the bag.

'Peoples **always** like dogs … never **kobolds** …'

'Would you care to come inside?' asked Nolin Sometimes, indicating the large treehouse that he'd started to run away from a few minutes before. 'There's not really space for a dragon, alas –' he grinned at Feathering – 'but there's a branch outside that should accommodate you close to the window. I could put on a fresh pot of tea while we discuss what has happened to the missing day?'

They agreed, and while they walked to the house Nolin Sometimes looked at Willow. His eyes went white, then blue, really fast. 'She came to live with you when you were five?'

Willow blinked. 'My grandmother?'

He nodded while Willow's eyes widened. 'Yes, when I was about five,' she said.

'She's quite difficult to manage since the accident

149

in the mountains, causing lots of arguments with your parents, is that right?'

'I'd prefer not to speak about that – thank you,' said Willow somewhat stiffly.

'Oh, yes, quite, sorry.'

A second later he started to laugh. 'Oho – she's going to be so mad when she finds out you took her favourite scarf!'

Clearly there were to be no secrets when you were around Nolin Sometimes.

'Did you run because you saw us?' asked Willow.

'Yes – I just run whenever I detect any humans approaching – saves time,' he admitted with a slightly embarrassed smile.

Willow wasn't sure if this was the best strategy to be honest, but then, considering what Moreg had said about forgotten tellers – mostly the bit about them winding up dead as a result of telling other people's secrets – *maybe not.*

The sun was beginning to set, turning the sky pink and purple and gold, and lanterns hanging magically in mid-air lit up as they neared the stilt house. On almost all the tree's branches were strange plants in pots, wind chimes and dangling objects that glinted in

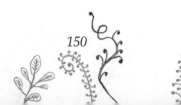

the lamp light. The clouds swirled to reveal that what Willow had thought were steps leading to the house were, in fact, rocks of various sizes suspended in the air at different heights.

She stepped up the rocks, trying her best not to look down. It was the strangest house she'd ever seen. Above the thin wooden stilts was a wide porch where odd-looking plants were hanging in pots, some of which seemed to have hair and others seemed to be looking straight back at her.

She followed Nolin Sometimes through the front door into a room where the walls were covered in botanical drawings and sketches, not unlike his childhood room. A long wooden desk dominated the room, which was cluttered with used teacups, feathers and strange devices that seemed to be humming. He touched a pink fluffy one now and it stopped, blinked and looked at Sometimes reproachfully with small raisin-like eyes. 'Furlarms,' he explained. 'They detect the approach of humans and other intruders.'

Willow noticed that there were apple-pie blossoms in a jar and she exclaimed in delight.

Nolin Sometimes looked pleased. 'You know these? They're quite rare; they sometimes grow on the tree –

quite harmless, well, for Wisperia. Try one.' So she did and they tasted just like warm apple pie.

In the corner of the room there was a small cheery kitchen with yellow wooden shelves. These held a rather impressive collection of teapots – at least a hundred that Willow could see – along with countless stacks of cups and saucers in shades of sky, plum and canary. She couldn't help wondering why one person would need so many. Next to a wide window was a wooden bed covered with a very lumpy and patchy blue-and-yellow quilt, where Nolin Sometimes put Harold down.

'Welcome,' he said, opening the window so that Feathering could peer inside from the branch where he'd perched.

'Pepper tea?' he asked the dragon.

'Ah yes, it's been centuries – I'd love a cup, if you don't mind?'

'It's no bother,' said Sometimes, fetching a bucket for Feathering, taking down a sky-coloured teapot and turning to go into the kitchen. There was a loud crash as the teapot shattered on the floor, followed by a thump as Nolin Sometimes keeled over backwards, his blue eyes suddenly white and cloudy.

'Not again!' cried Willow, rushing over to kneel

beside him and trying to wake him up.

'What's happened?' cried Feathering, trying to peer through the window, his large golden eye filling up most of the frame.

'He's fainted again!'

Harold roused himself off the bed, unsticking his tongue from the coverlet with some effort. He landed with a thud and proceeded to howl at the sight of Nolin Sometimes's prone figure surrounded by shards of broken crockery – which at least explained why he had so many teapots.

'It's all right, Harold,' said Willow, patting the dog.

**''Tis not all right!'** harrumphed Oswin. **'We'll *starve* at this rate.'**

It was a full minute before Sometimes stirred, then he shouted, 'CAPTURED!' and sat up very fast to look at Willow, which was incredibly eerie as his eyes were still pure white. Suddenly his eyes changed back to blue and his hands started tearing at his wild white hair.

'Moreg Vaine was CAPTURED BY THE BROTHERS OF WOL? You don't think you could have mentioned that *FROM THE START?*'

Willow's mouth gaped open. 'Oh. Um . . . yes,' she conceded. 'I was just getting to that part . . .'

153

Nolin Sometimes's eyes were nearly popping their sockets. 'Tuesday has gone missing. Stolen, most likely, which could make our world unravel bit by bit, and the most powerful witch in Starfell has been taken prisoner, which means . . .'

He looked at her, then at Feathering.

Willow nodded. 'There's just us to get it back and save the world, yes.'

'I was afraid you were going to say that.'

Sometimes fell away into a faint once again.

Willow sighed and started clearing up the debris. It's what she did. She'd come from a home where everyone else had always been far too busy being self-important for chores. Chores were her thing.

She took down a new teapot, yellow this time, feeling the need for a cheering sort of colour, picked up the fallen bucket and then filled it with pepper tea for Feathering. She spied some weren leaves and decided to pop them in the teapot for Sometimes – weren flowers were known for their calming properties.

She placed the bucket of tea on a branch for the dragon, who eyed it with pleasure. 'Just the thing – I've had a terrible cold,' he said, taking a sip.

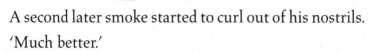

A second later smoke started to curl out of his nostrils.
'Much better.'

She took a sip of the weren tea and sat down in an
armchair. From within the bag she could hear Oswin
slurping the cup she'd passed him. Harold, it seemed,
had decided to go back to bed.

Sometimes sat up and rubbed his head. 'I can't believe she's been captured,' he lamented, carrying on his conversation as if a full ten minutes hadn't just passed, coming to sit opposite Willow in one of the armchairs.

Willow blinked. 'Ah – yes, unfortunately.'

'But how?' he cried.

'Well, we were entering the city of Bead—'

'Beady Hill, yes, and then the High Master arrived!'

She frowned. 'Oh, you saw that? Well, they had these magical—'

He nodded impatiently. 'Manacles, yes – but she could get out of those if she wanted!'

'Yes,' said Willow slowly with a frown. Obviously he could just see her memory of the event for himself.

He looked from her to Feathering. 'What I mean is – *how* was *Moreg Vaine* captured? How could she have let it happen? Surely she could have fought them off?'

'Is she very powerful?' asked Feathering.

Willow nodded, thinking of how thunder and lightning had ripped the sky. 'I don't think that they could really have captured her without her consent. I don't know why she allowed it. I really don't.

But what I do know is that *this* was her plan. She wanted me to come here and find you –' she looked at him now – 'she thought that perhaps you could help.'

His eyes popped. 'Me?'

She nodded. 'She said that until we found out *who* took the day I couldn't try to summon it – not until we know what we're dealing with first.'

He blinked a few times. Then his eyes went hazy and he sank into a faint.

She sighed, took a sip of tea and shrugged at Feathering.

**'Bonkers,'** said Oswin, who'd opened the bag, and was leaning against the dragon egg, his legs crossed.

Sometimes sat bolt upright. 'YOU ALMOST ENDED THE WORLD?'

He was obviously recalling the moment when she tried to summon the day and Moreg Vaine started to panic.

Outside Feathering boomed, 'WHAT?' in shock. 'You almost ended the world?'

Willow shrugged. 'Only almost.'

She explained that if she'd brought the day into the current reality it might have split apart the fabric

of time. 'See, that's why I can't try to find it just yet – we need to know who took it and why first. So, can you tell us who took last Tuesday?' she asked Nolin Sometimes.

He rubbed his head and sighed deeply. He took a sip of his cold tea, then said, 'It's just not clear, and what I'm getting, well, it doesn't make any sense!'

'Oh?' said Willow.

Feathering looked just as surprised. 'What are you getting?' he asked.

'Something impossible – I mean, they said they were all destroyed; no one has been able to find one to even try, but . . .'

'What?'

He stood up and started pacing the floor. As he spoke he spilled tea from his cup, which trailed along with his steps. 'Well, I just keep seeing the oddest thing whenever I try to look at last Tuesday specifically. I see one thing, and I keep seeing it.' He gesticulated with his hands, making more tea jump wildly out of his cup. 'Which is strange because usually there's so much – too much really – to see. But it's like this great big emptiness and then beyond all of that it's white, and in the distance there's something handwritten and

very old hidden in a small gilt box inside a guarded fortress.'

'Like a letter?' asked Willow.

Sometimes looked at her. 'No – like a spell. *A Lost Spell.*'

# 11

## The Lost Spells of Starfell

Willow gaped at Sometimes. It wasn't possible. It couldn't be. It was myth. Legend.

'But the Lost Spells were destroyed during the war a thousand years ago!' she exclaimed.

Sometimes shook his head. 'Not all of them *apparently.*'

Willow's mind filled with wonder. Growing up, she'd heard the stories about the old magicians of Starfell, and the legends about the Lost Spells. Who hadn't? The first time she was told about what happened to the old magicians was not long after she'd discovered her own magical ability – and was a bit upset about it.

*'Stop your crying, child. Don't you know how lucky you are?' scoffed Granny Flossy, putting down her*

glass of sherry and managing to look serious despite her lime-green hair.

Six-year-old Willow sniffed. 'Lucky?' she said, looking at her in disbelief. Her almond eyes filled with tears again. 'They call me Fetch – even Mum! By my age Camille could move the whole kitchen with her mind – and what can I do? Find socks?' she wailed.

'It's hardly just socks. You found my toothbrush last week,' Granny Flossy pointed out.

Willow didn't think that was any better. She sniffed, then looked down at the floor. 'It's not really special . . .'

'So what? It's still magic – it's still a gift. Not everyone can do what you can.'

Willow scoffed. 'It's not like Juniper's magic or Camille's.'

Granny Flossy looked at her hard, then shook her head, seeming disappointed. 'I thought you were more sensible, child. Don't you realise that you are one of the lucky ones? I mean, the very fact that you've even got magic at all is incredible. After the battles we fought? The war we almost lost? How many people died, how long it took for magic to re-enter Starfell – and yet you scoff at what you have?'

Willow's mouth fell open in surprise. 'People died?'

'Yes, hundreds – thousands even. It was a different world. Back then magic ran freely throughout Starfell, and those who used it were great wizards and witches called magicians, who could do incredibly powerful things. Some of them had several magical gifts at once.'

Willow blinked. 'Really?'

Granny Flossy nodded.

'What happened?'

'The Brothers of Wol were scared of those old magicians – the ones who could do anything with magic, anything they wanted – and that was the problem, you see.'

'What do you mean?'

'They were afraid. I think most people felt fear – even today people are always a bit scared of what they can't understand. Things that are different. But it wasn't until the Brothers of Wol started telling people that magic was unnatural, that it wasn't a gift from the god of light, Wol, but from the dark god, Mal, that fear really started to spread in people's hearts.

'Soon enough, the Brothers told the people that

they needed to rid Starfell of this evil. At this time Starfell was united under one ruler, a king, and he became convinced that he must act. All magic was forbidden, especially the writing down of spells, as he and the Brothers of Wol feared that these spells could destroy them all. But, in a last attempt to preserve thousands of years of magic, the magicians gathered the best of their spells and hid them in the hope they would never be lost.'

'Did it work?'

'No. The Brothers of Wol found out and it led to war. They believed that those with magic had gathered these spells together in order to attack those without, and they persuaded the king to strike first. Thousands died as a result and during the battle the spells were said to have been destroyed.'

'But couldn't the old magicians just fight back – use the magic that people were so afraid of?'

'Some did, yes, but fear is a powerful force. The Brothers of Wol captured their families and threatened to kill them if they fought back. Many of the people they captured weren't magical. As you know, not everyone in a family is born with magic, so they couldn't fight back even if they tried.'

163

Willow thought of her father and nodded. She thought of what she'd do if someone captured him and threatened to hurt him – probably anything they asked her to, she realised.

'Then there were those with magic who betrayed their own kind – that was the worst part,' sighed Granny Flossy, taking a sip of her sherry and staring off into the distance. 'You see some of them started to believe that what the Brothers said was true – that it was an evil gift. They were told that Wol would take away their sins if they worked to rid the world of this evil, so they helped the Brothers to destroy their own kind.'

Willow was horrified. 'But why would they believe that?'

Granny Flossy grabbed Willow's face, looked deep in her eyes and said, 'Fear, my girl. It's more powerful than any magic in this world. It's what's holding you back right now – the fear that you won't be as powerful as your sisters, the fear that your gift isn't special. But it is. You think your powers aren't exciting? Well, I think that you're wrong. Magic is like life – it's what you do with it that counts. The Brothers of Wol tried everything to rid Starfell of

*magic, but they couldn't do it. It still came back to our world, slowly but surely, after all those centuries. And now, years later, a small piece of it found you. It singled you out and made you special. Never forget that, my girl – the fact that you have a magical ability at all is proof of how lucky you really are.'*

Willow looked at Nolin Sometimes now, her eyes wide. She'd half convinced herself that the Lost Spells were nothing more than myth – just a story about the old magicians of Starfell.

'You really think someone has found one of them?'

'Yes – and if there's one, there might be others.'

**'That jes can't be good,'** said Oswin.

Feathering's golden eye had widened. 'I can't help but agree . . .'

Nolin Sometimes nodded.

Willow blinked. 'But even if one of those old, powerful spells had survived, surely it wouldn't work? I mean, there are no magicians *left*, right? Could a witch or wizard use one of those old spells now?'

Sometimes frowned. 'Maybe . . . The magic was here before. You can't erase it, and long ago our ancestors could use them, so perhaps we could too.

I'm not sure. But I think that there might be at least one who *can*, someone who found a way to get some of the old powers back . . .'

Willow's eyes bulged. 'You mean to find the missing Tuesday we're going to have to fight someone who has managed to tap into the old powers? Someone as powerful as one of the old magicians of Starfell?'

Sometimes looked a little green himself. 'I'm afraid so.'

## 12

## The Moon Garden

'But who? Who is this magician? Can you see him?' asked Willow.

Nolin Sometimes ran a hand through his wild white hair, and shook his head. 'No, but I think I know a way that we can find out.'

Willow looked from Feathering perched outside the window, his large golden eye blinking rapidly at the news, to Oswin, and asked, 'Really? How?'

Nolin Sometimes grinned. 'As you may know, I am also a botanist.'

'Um?' said Willow.

Oswin blinked. **'I tol' yew 'e's off his rocker,'** he said.

Nolin Sometimes's passion for botany explained the strange plants dotted around the stilt house and how they'd come to find him in the magical forest

of Wisperia, but not, Willow couldn't help thinking, how it might help them understand who had taken the missing Tuesday.

Sometimes sighed dramatically, shaking his head. 'The study of botany, along with the art of forgotten telling, have long been entwined. The early oubliers were able to grow certain plants that helped them in telling larger portions of the past. The roots of these plants connect beneath the ground, creating a large network of memory, and if we can access the right ones, we can find out what really happened. Do you understand?' he said rather excitedly.

Willow, Oswin and Feathering all shook their heads.

Sometimes sighed again. 'Plants are not just pretty things that grow waiting for our fingers to pluck at them, you know? They are smarter than we realise and many are able to warn each other in times of danger. Some are always listening to what we have to say, and, if you get the right one, you can find out anything you wish to know.'

Willow's mouth plopped open in shock. '*Really?*'

Nolin Sometimes nodded.

Willow would never think of plants the same way again.

168

'Can all forgotten tellers find out the secrets of plants?' she asked.

Sometimes's face drooped, and he took a sip of his now stone-cold tea, his blue eyes sad. 'Not any more. It's a bit hard to keep up with gardening while you're running for your life,' he said with a rueful grin. 'Only a few of us have got the old skills. I'm one of the lucky ones; my grandfather taught me all he knew. And on his deathbed he gave me a small box that contained the seeds of one of the most special plants ever grown – the memory flower. This flower will reveal one secret under the light of the moon before it dies.'

Willow and Feathering quickly looked up at the darkening sky, where they could see a crescent moon peeking out through the clouds.

'That's right,' continued Sometimes. 'It will bloom soon.'

At nightfall, using a set of stairs along the side of the swaying stilt house, Willow followed Sometimes. She had left Oswin behind in the house with Harold, much to the kobold's annoyance. 'I can't carry you to the roof,' she'd said to his orange back. 'You know you

could just walk with us?' she'd added. But there had been a disgruntled sniff and he'd shot her a look of disbelief over his shoulder, then went back to sulking, paws crossed over his chest. Clearly staying inside, even if it was with a *dog*, was preferable to having to go outside or leave the comfort of the hairy carpetbag.

Up and up they continued to climb, towards the roof of the house.

'Don't worry, she's as sturdy as a rock,' said Sometimes as the house gave a rather terrifying jolt to the side and then righted itself.

Willow's hands shook, but she managed somehow to get to the top, where she found herself in a very unusual garden. Perched among the clouds it was laid out in various patterns of concentric circles. Eagerly Willow darted forward to have a look at the sorts of plants that would go into a 'moon garden'. Rather disappointingly, though, they were all the same rather dull brown shade, with leaves that drooped on to the ground. They looked pretty dead really.

'It's interesting,' she managed as a response to Sometimes's rather expectant look.

Sometimes laughed. 'It doesn't look like much now – but just wait. Unlike normal daytime plants these ones only show their glory during the light of the moon,' he explained.

'It's hard to imagine these having any glory,' said Feathering, joining them, his massive feathered bulk swaying in the clouds.

Sometimes shook his head, a smile playing about his lips. 'You'll see.'

It didn't take long. As the moonlight stretched across the garden the plants began to transform. They grew larger, their leaves changing shape – some with vivid stripes and others with splotches of paint-like drips on their leaves – and magnificent flowers in shades of super-bright white, sunshine, topaz and electric pinks, blues and purples sprouted in the glowing moonlight.

'They're amazing!' Willow said as she reached out to touch the soft, furry petals of one at her feet. She gasped when the plant reached out to touch her back.

'The scent,' said Feathering, closing his large golden eye in apparent bliss. 'Like a fresh, juicy deer on a clear mountain path after the storm.'

Willow closed her eyes and breathed in. 'I smell hot chocolate with cinnamon and marshmallows!'

Sometimes grinned. 'That's a bliss flower; it produces the scent of what you most enjoy!'

Feathering hovered above the clouds, his powerful wings beating the air, making Willow's hair blow back. 'So one of these will tell us who took the missing Tuesday?' he asked.

'Yes,' said Sometimes. 'This one,' he said, coming to a stop in the centre of the garden, where a tall pale-green plant surrounded by a circle of white pebbles

was slowly beginning to transform.

It was bigger than the others, but less colourful. While they watched the green leaves began to open very slowly and a tall, thin stem appeared. Translucent like glass, the stem unfurled and a large pure-white flower emerged, its tiny fronds covered in what looked like gold dust. Its petals opened and it shifted ever so slightly towards Nolin Sometimes and bowed its petal head.

An expectant hush descended. Sometimes touched it, then asked, 'Tell us, Memory Flower, who took last Tuesday?'

Willow held her breath.

The flower began to shift, its petals unfurling outwards, twisting and growing, and changing before their eyes into the shape of a young man. His form was made of airy lace-like petals. There were holes where his eyes should have been, and his hair was made of the same golden thread that had covered the fronds of the memory flower. He was wearing a long robe with what looked like golden arrows in the centre.

The plant boy looked at them with eyes that weren't there and said in a voice like wind rattling

a doorframe, *'The boy called Silas cast the spell hidden within the fortress.'*

'A fortress?' cried Willow. 'Which fortress? Which spell? How can we get it back?'

The plant boy shook his head, and before their eyes he began to disappear, turning back into a flower once more. Then each of the flower's petals scattered to the wind.

Sometimes sighed. 'Like I said, you only get the one question.' He turned to look at Willow. 'At least we know *who* to look for now.'

Willow nodded. Someone called Silas. 'And that it *was* a spell.'

'Which means that you won't be able to summon the lost day,' said Sometimes.

'Why not?' asked Willow.

'The magic of the spell might react to your own when you summon it; it could do what Moreg feared and split apart the universe,' explained Sometimes.

Willow blinked, put aside the part of her mind that was panicking in Oswin's voice, and going *'Oh noooo,'* and thought hard. 'What if I tried to summon the spell?'

Sometimes contemplated the idea. 'Hmm, yes,

perhaps there is a counter-spell on the scroll. If it worked for whoever used it to take away the day, perhaps it could work for one of us too. Like I said, the old magic was here before, so if we found some of it, it's possible we could still use it. I'm not sure, though.'

Willow had to at least try. It was worth trying to summon the spell scroll in any case. She closed her eyes and raised her hand to the sky. All she had to do was try to find it. It was a *lost* spell after all. She concentrated hard. But it would not come. It was as if somehow something was blocking her from getting it.

'It's no good – I feel it, but it won't come.'

Sometimes gasped, perhaps as if he too realised something at the same time she did.

She opened her eyes and whispered, '*Practical makes perfect.*'

Had it been Moreg's plan all along?

'Pardon?' asked Feathering.

Sometimes's eyes went blank and he keeled over.

Willow explained. 'I think I know which fortress the memory flower was referring to. I tried to summon the spell but I couldn't. It was like something was blocking me, and I think I know why. It's because

the spell is in the one place in all of Starfell that can't be penetrated with magic: Wolkana. The monastery of the Brothers of Wol. It's a *fortress*. And the only way a witch can get inside is—'

'If she gets *captured*,' said Sometimes, sitting up. His eyes were going blue once more and he sounded awed. 'Moreg meant to be! It was part of her plan!'

'*Practical makes perfect*,' repeated Willow. 'It makes sense – she *wanted* them to take her so she could get inside!'

'But how does that help us?' asked Feathering. 'If we can't get inside? Can a dragon?'

Sometimes shook his head. 'I think Wolkana is sealed off from all magical creatures.'

Willow blinked. 'Maybe not.' Something had just occurred to her.

'What do you mean?' asked Sometimes.

She grinned at them. 'Moreg said whenever she's lost she *looks inside her pantry* and that's where she finds the answers . . .'

They all looked blank, so she continued. 'Moreg's cloak – which she was wearing when they took her – it's a portal to the pantry in her home. If we can get inside that pantry, we can get to her!'

'Brilliant, absolutely brilliant,' said Nolin Sometimes.

'So can you show us the way to Moreg's house?' Willow asked Sometimes.

'Hmm, I was afraid you were going to say that,' said Sometimes, before he keeled over backwards again.

Willow fished the StoryPass out of her pocket. The needle was currently aimed at *Turning Point*. It then swung around to point to *'One Might Have Suspected as Such'*, and she sighed.

'I wish he'd stop that,' said Feathering. 'This is no time to fall apart.'

Willow looked from the StoryPass to Nolin Sometimes's still form, then said, 'I think that's the problem, you see . . .'

'None of us know where it is,' agreed Sometimes, sitting up and rubbing his head.

'How is that possible?' asked Feathering, incredulous.

Willow stared. 'Well, she is Moreg Vaine, you know?'

The dragon just stared. 'Oh, yes, quite.'

'She's the most powerful witch in Starfell. There are rumours about where she lives . . .'

'Some say it's in the Mists of Mitlaire, or the Lake of the Undead,' agreed Willow.

'But the truth is, no one really knows,' continued Sometimes. 'And she's fiercely secretive; it's not like she has friends we can just go and ask—' He turned to look at Willow, then his eyes went pale and white.

'Except, what if she does?' Willow finished for him, guessing he'd just seen her memory of when Moreg had first come to her cottage. 'Moreg told me that long ago she and my mother were friends. That they grew up together in Ditchwater . . . What if my mum knows where she lives?'

Sometimes started muttering to himself. 'I'll just have to let Harold know that I might be gone for a while. He's capable of feeding himself . . . and I doubt he'd be up for the journey . . . anyway. It's Sunday night, so the fair is probably at the Midnight Market now . . .' Sometimes turned to Willow. 'Looks like we're going to have to go to the Travelling Fortune Fair,' he said.

Willow didn't bother asking him how he knew where her mother was or what the next stop on the travelling fair was likely to be – he must have read her memories. Her stomach plummeted in sudden

fear at the thought of facing her family and having to explain why she'd lied . . . and why she was now in the company of a dragon and a forgotten teller. 'I was afraid you were going to say that.'

# 13

## The Midnight Market

Under cover of darkness Feathering set Willow and her friends down in a wooded valley close to the Midnight Market, which was one of the stops of the Travelling Fortune Fair. Landing in a valley a little away from the market had been Willow's idea as she'd pictured the screams of terror that arriving in the centre of the fair on a dragon may have caused.

Admittedly, for one glorious second, she had also pictured the look on Camille and Juniper's shocked faces when they saw her on the back of the dragon . . . But then she had decided, somewhat regretfully, that doing so wouldn't help their ultimate cause.

'I'll wait here for your return,' said Feathering.

'Me too,' said Oswin, using a paw to cover a yawn, and turning over inside the hairy carpetbag.

Willow shot him A Look, then picked up the hairy

bag, and he grumbled, '**Why** does 'e get to stay?'

'Because Feathering is a *dragon* – and therefore really hard to disguise. You, however, are not. You're coming with me.'

There was a harrumph, but he agreed. Mainly because she promised him something to eat along the way.

Hairy bag in hand, Willow and Sometimes followed the sound of people's voices, the scent of wood fires and the twinkling lights until they'd found the Midnight Market.

String lights cast their amber beams on tents of all shapes, sizes and colours. People weaved in and out, their arms filled with goods they'd bought or traded. Many of the goods looked dangerous, or deadly . . . the sort of thing you might expect only to get at midnight . . . There were curly wots' tails, which, if slipped inside a bed, found their way on to a person's neck and began to strangle them, and glass flowers that had a strange sweet scent that could put someone into an enchanted sleep forevermore.

Willow passed two women who were having a heated argument. 'I don't know what you're playing at, Gardelia, I never took your money. Even if I can't

recall right now what I did last Tuesday, that doesn't mean I took your purse . . .'

'Yes it does!' screeched the other woman, red in the face. 'I saw you eyeing it on Monday – and it's now missing, so you must have!'

Near to one of the bigger tents a wizard with purple dreadlocks, wearing multi-coloured trousers was intoning, '*Heva spice, heva spice! Throw it at your enemies, blast them off their feet!*'

'This place is a little dodgy, isn't it?' said Willow. 'Can't believe this is one of my mother's stops . . .'

There was a sound like 'Mimble mumble,' and she turned and saw that Nolin Sometimes's eyes had gone all white and glassy, and he was just about to pass out in a dead faint. 'Oh no!' cried Willow, catching him.

'**Absolutely** bonkers,' said Oswin, looking out from the hole within the bag.

'It must be all the people – all their memories!' guessed Willow. 'Now what am I going to do?'

'I'll tell you what you're going to do,' came a rather familiar voice from behind, a voice that caused Willow's ears to burn a bright red. 'You are going to explain what on Great Starfell you are doing here.'

Willow turned round slowly. A tall, stern-looking

witch dressed in maroon and gold with several shawls across her shoulders stood with her arms crossed. She had long black hair down to her waist, golden hoop earrings and blazing green eyes.

Willow cringed. 'Hello, Mum.'

A few minutes later, Willow was being dragged into the back of her mother's large red-and-gold travelling wagon. Her sister Camille, meanwhile, had moved Nolin Sometimes to the guard's tent with her mind.

Facing Willow, Camille crowed. 'Ooooh, you're in for it now . . . Dad sent a raven asking if Mum had lost her mind taking you along to the fair . . . and of course she hadn't!'

'Enough, Camille!' said her mother, holding up a hand. Her green eyes flashed fire. 'Your sister is right, though. We've been worried sick! You left your father a note saying you were joining us – why? And where have you been? Why did you leave the cottage? Who was that old man? Explain yourself,' she said, crossing her arms.

'He's not an old man!'

Willow's mother's nostrils flared. 'Fine, the man with the white hair then. Who. Is. He?'

Willow sat in a small chair across from her mother and sisters, took a deep breath and tried to explain. 'I. Well. You see, Moreg Vaine came to the cottage, looking for help.'

185

'*Moreg Vaine* came to our cottage?' scoffed Camille.

'YES.'

Her oldest sister, Juniper, looked incredulous too, but she tried to understand. 'Really? But why?'

Juniper and Camille started speaking at once. But their mother held up a hand for silence. 'She was looking for me?' she asked. 'Why didn't you just send a raven? I could have come back, or she could have met up with us on the road?'

Willow shook her head. 'Um, no – she came looking for me.'

'You?' said Juniper. Her eyebrows shot up into her hairline.

Camille laughed. 'Moreg Vaine came to look for you? What was wrong? She'd lost her marbles?' She sniggered.

Her mother shot Camille a look, and she stopped sniggering at once. 'Go on,' she said, though it was clear she too was struggling to believe Willow.

Willow frowned. 'She needed my help. It's last Tuesday. You see, well, it's gone missing and she needed me to help find it.'

'*Last Tuesday has gone missing,*' repeated her mother, somewhat incredulously. She turned back to

Willow, breathing heavily. 'And where is Moreg now? Can she confirm this at all?'

'You can't tell me you believe this story—' said Camille.

Her mother shot her another silencing look.

Willow continued. 'She – well, she got arrested.'

'**Arrested!**' Juniper exclaimed.

Camille gasped. 'The most powerful witch in Starfell arrested?' She started to snigger, and Juniper joined in.

Their mother looked at Willow, her expression sad. 'Willow, I know you think that I don't take you with me because I don't want you with me, but that is just not true. You are too young to be here. But you didn't need to make up some far-fetched tale to get yourself here.'

Willow stood up. They were wasting time. 'I'm not lying!'

An angry bright-orange fur-covered head popped out of the carpetbag and growled. '**Oi!** Yeh **cackling hens,** she's telling **the truth!**'

187

Camille's eyes widened, disgust smeared across her face. 'You brought that – that *thing* along with you? I mean, I thought I smelt something horrid, but I assumed it was just you . . .'

Willow's eyes flashed. 'He's more useful than you. At least he listens.'

Willow's mother pinched the bridge of her nose and took a deep breath. 'If that were remotely true, I'm sure we'd notice that the day was missing—'

'But just think – what were you doing on Tuesday? Please, Mum, you'll see what I mean.'

Willow's mother closed her eyes, then shook her head sadly. 'Willow, I'm disappointed in you. I've never taken you for a liar before.'

Camille smirked at this, and Willow fought the urge to scream. Her mother continued. 'We still have

188

a few things to finish up here before we go home tomorrow morning,' she said, her mouth in a thin line. 'So for tonight you will stay with a friend of mine. In the morning I will take you home myself.'

Willow's mouth fell open. Why wouldn't she just believe her? 'No – please you must understand! We have to save Tuesday – I have to find Moreg's house – you're the only one who knows where she lives. That's why we came here. Mum, I really need to do this. If we don't, it could mean the end of the world.'

There was silence. Then Camille and Juniper burst out laughing again.

'Can you believe this? *"The end of the world"*! She's lost it, honestly,' scoffed Camille.

Willow's mother shook her head, muttering to her sisters. 'I blame myself. Left her alone too much with your crazy grandmother, and now look . . .' She broke off, looking a bit sad.

Ten minutes later, Willow found herself in the home of her mother's friend Rubix, who seemed to take the craft a bit *too seriously*. The house was shaped like a pentagram, and everything in it from the stove to the sofa and the kitchen table was made to fit precisely

into each point and nook and cranny of the star-shaped house. The walls were a pleasing blue and sunset pink, a bit like a galaxy. There were even little speckles of stars all over the floors.

Sitting across from Willow was a rather short girl of around her own age, who was wearing a nightgown that was at least two sizes too big. She had very long curly hair, pretty skin the colour of a hazelnut, and large round glasses that rested on the edge of a small button nose. Next to her was a black cat, who was eying Willow's hairy suitcase with some interest.

Oswin was currently muttering *'Oh noooo,'* though rather softly.

'This is Essential Jones,' introduced Rubix. 'I'm afraid I have to dash off – need to get some ratwort from the market – but Essential here will make up a bed for you. Mind you two go straight to sleep.' She gave Willow a kindly look as she continued. 'At your mother's request I've put a charm on the door – just in case you try to escape, you understand.' And with that she left.

The girl was eyeing Willow with interest, her brown eyes huge behind the frames. 'So, you're one of Raine Moss's children?'

Willow nodded, her face a bit glum. 'Yes. Not one of the ones you would have heard about, though.'

Essential shrugged. 'Still, to come from a family of witches, that's something. I was the first one in mine for ages . . . That's why I was sent to Rubix – the law, you know,' she said with a small shrug.

Willow looked puzzled, so Essential explained. 'Well, if no one in your family has a magical ability and one of your children develops a fizz of magic, the law is that they have to be sent to someone who can help them control it. So I was sent here just after I was born, to Rubix, as she was the closest witch. My mother was really upset – not only because I was sent away, but because after five boys I was the only girl. See, that's how I got my name. My mother said, "You can't take my girl, she's *essential*." And Rubix took it a bit literally.'

Willow grinned. Then frowned. Something Moreg had said before she was taken by the Brothers of Wol floated in her mind.

The witch had said, '*Remember, practical makes perfect . . . And, when you think of it, a little rain is essential for uncovering what you might need.*'

Willow jumped out of her chair. Unless she'd meant *Raine* and *Essential* – as in two people.

'I think I was meant to find you!'

Essential stared at her as if she'd gone mad.

Willow fished the StoryPass from within her pocket. The needle was currently pointed to '*One Might Have Suspected as Such*', and she grinned.

Essential blinked. 'You were meant to find me?'

She nodded. 'I think that's what Moreg Vaine wanted.'

Essential was still frowning, so Willow explained about everything and how they needed to find Moreg's house.

'Moreg said she knew my mother – Raine. Which is why I came here, because I thought my mother would be able to tell me where Moreg's house is – but maybe she also wanted me to find you – something *Essential*.'

Essential blinked. 'But . . . but I'm nothing special. I mean, I can't do much besides freeze things and that's only for about a second, if it's going slow enough.'

'Freeze things?'

Essential turned to the cat who was licking his paw and flung out her hand. The next second the cat froze, mid-lick, his tongue sticking out at them.

Essential gave a rueful sort of grin. 'It's a bit hit and miss to be honest. If I'm upset, it's a bit more powerful. Once I stopped a bucket of water from being thrown at me when I was walking outside. I mean, it was just for a second; I still got drenched, and I got this,' she said, lifting her hair and showing Willow a scar, which was shiny and pale against her dark skin, on the side of her head where the bucket had hit her.

Willow shrugged. 'Maybe that's enough. I'm nobody special – I mean, all I do is find lost things – socks mostly, or wallets and keys. Maybe you don't need big magic to save the world? Maybe you've just got to be willing to try?'

Essential nodded, and then stood up. 'Okay.'

'So you'll help me?'

Essential nodded, pushing up her glasses, and grinned. 'Yes.' Then she stopped. 'Well, um, let me just get out of my nightgown first.'

When she returned she was dressed in a black dress with little gold moons and silver stars all over it that Willow couldn't help admiring.

'Ready.' Willow smiled.

'Ready.' Essential nodded.

But when they tried the door, just as Rubix had warned, it was charmed shut.

'Now what?' cried Willow.

# 14

## The Hag Stone

It wasn't just the door; the windows were locked too. Nothing would budge, and even when Willow tried breaking one of the panes of glass with a large cast-iron pot from the kitchen nothing happened. It didn't even crack.

Essential sighed. 'It's all been charmed shut. That's Rubix's gift – she can charm objects to do what she wants.'

Willow frowned, her eyes huge. 'But we need to get out of here! I've got to find Nolin Sometimes, try to get him awake. Hopefully he'll be able to read my mother's memories so that we can find Moreg's house!'

Oswin cleared his throat, like he was trying to get her attention, but Willow was distracted when Essential suddenly smacked her forehead. 'I have an

195

idea!' she cried, dashing away to fetch something from inside her bedroom.

Oswin reached out a paw and tapped her hand. 'Not now, Oswin,' she said as Essential came back into the room holding an ordinary black stone with a hole in its centre.

'It's a hag stone,' she explained, a grin splitting apart her face.

'A hag stone?'

There was a huff from the bag and some dark muttering.

Essential raised a brow and Willow mouthed, 'Don't ask.'

Essential shrugged. 'Yes. It can help you see things that are magic – things that pretend otherwise. *But it can also undo charms* – especially magic that has already been cast, like Rubix's charm to shut the door!' She looked at Willow and shook her head. 'Actually, you'll never guess who I got it from! Something you said reminded me of it . . . even though I've had it for about four years . . . I mean, it's not like I needed it with Rubix; she can cast off charms too . . .'

Willow raised a brow. 'Moreg Vaine?' she guessed.

Essential nodded. 'She gave it to me at a fair – said

that it might come in handy one day. I mean, it was Moreg Vaine, so of course I kept it, but I'd sort of forgotten about it till now.'

'But can it work if we're inside the locked house?'

There was a snort from within the bag.

'I'm not sure,' said Essential, eyeing the bag a bit warily, then she looked through the hole, while Willow tested the door. Nothing changed; it was still locked. She handed the stone to Willow who looked through the hole herself, then while holding it she tried the door.

Nothing.

''**Ag stones don' work** inside a charm,' came Oswin's exasperated voice from the hairy bag. '**Everyone who isn't a cumberworld knows that.**'

Essential was looking at the bag in some shock.

'Oh,' said Willow. She sighed. 'Now what are we going to do?'

'**Well,**' drawled Oswin, peeking out of the bag now that she'd stopped ignoring him. '**If you'd asks me, which you din't, I would 'ave said that yew could jes climb out o' the chimonemuney there. I don't fink the charm reaches that far,**' he said, a now orange paw pointing to the chimney.

197

Willow and Essential shared a look. They tested it, finding that Oswin was right; it wasn't charmed shut. 'Ah yes. That's probably the best idea,' said Essential, turning slightly pink.

'Thanks, Oswin,' said Willow.

Five minutes later, with the help of a ladder and some hefting and pulling, Willow and Essential – and Oswin – made it through on to the roof. From there they jumped on to the soft grass below, the bag landing with a bit of a thump, which caused Oswin to swear in High Dwarf.

'This is Oswin, by the way,' said Willow, introducing him to Essential as he muttered darkly about missing his stove and wondering what he was doing in a bag made of hair agreeing to come on some crazy adventure.

'Why are you inside that bag anyway?' interrupted Essential, who was curious about him.

He stopped grumbling. '**Because I's a kobold, and the monster from under the bed . . . At least I used to be. Now I'm the monster in the bag, which jes don' have quite the same rings to it,**' he said with a sigh, as he ventured half a head out of the zipped bag to peer at her.

Essential brightened. 'A kobold, wow – I hear they can blow things up.'

'**Only** when **we** is really, *really* **cross,**' said Oswin, who seemed to have warmed to Essential. He hadn't turned completely orange at least.

'Happens a lot,' whispered Willow. Then she said more loudly, 'Right. We need to find Nolin Sometimes – my mother said he was taken to the guard's tent.'

Essential nodded. 'I know it. Come on,' she said, and they raced through the dark woods, looking over their shoulders in case anyone was keeping an eye out for them – particularly Willow's sisters. After a while they entered the edge of the clearing and they could see the many coloured tents of the fair and the rows of string lights suspended above them.

They darted behind tents, crouching down low, and Essential said, 'It's the big red-and-white one, there.' She pointed to the end of the clearing. As they neared they could hear raised voices coming from within the tent.

'WHO TOLD YOU THAT?'

'No one told me,' said Nolin Sometimes in a small, tired voice.

'SOMEONE'S PUT YOU UP TO THIS, HAVEN'T THEY? WAS IT BILL?'

'Look, I can understand that you're upset about your, er . . . most likely former business partner now, but, um, can you keep it down? I have a bit of a headache, you see. Also . . . incidentally, it *was* Bill, though he never told me exactly . . . but I mean how could you not have seen that he painted those chicken eggs gold?'

'WOT YOU MEAN! HOW'D YER KNOW IT THEN? HUH, 'SPLAIN THAT?'

'SO YOU ADMIT IT THEN, BILL! YOU LYING CROOK!'

Willow and Essential entered the tent to see two very angry guards glaring at each other.

'Um, hello?' said Willow.

They looked up, but carried on arguing.

Willow ran up to Sometimes, who sagged in relief when he saw her. 'Who is this?' he asked as she untied his hands.

'Never mind, I'll explain later,' she said, tugging him along.

But he stopped, his eyes

going white, then back to blue in a blink, and he muttered, his voice high and girly, *'Freddy Slimespoon has eyes like drops of dew on a toad-filled grass. With a smile like the blissful morning sunshine ballooning through a crack of window and bouncing against the starry walls of my heart . . .'*

Essential stared from him to Willow, utterly mortified. 'Um,' she squeaked, 'how does he know about that?' Her eyes were huge. 'I was very young, well, younger, um, when I wrote that poem . . . I don't know how you found it . . .'

Willow rolled her eyes. They didn't have time for this. 'C'mon,' she said, but it was too late – they'd been spotted.

The two guards cried out. 'Stop! Wait there just a minute!'

'Essential!' cried Willow. 'Freeze them!'

She whirled round and froze the guards mid-stride.

'Run!' yelled Essential.

The freeze wore off almost instantly but it gave them just enough time to dash into the crowd. Nolin Sometimes had his hands over his ears and was going 'Lalalalalalala.'

'What are you doing?' asked Willow.

201

'What?' he bellowed, his hair wild and crackling with electricity, his blue eyes enormous.

'What are you doing?' she repeated.

'Blocking them out – so I don't have to hear their memories.'

But it was too late, as soon as he'd focused on Willow his eyes went all glassy and white and the next second he was keeling over backwards.

'Oh no! Not again!' cried Willow.

'What's happened?' asked Essential.

Willow explained. 'He's an oublier – a forgotten teller – he has what he calls "visions", which let him see the past but make him pass out . . . and with all the people here, well, it's a bit too much for him, I think.'

Willow spied a very small tent that looked like it was still being erected. It sagged in the middle and one of the poles was on its side.

She jerked her head towards it. 'Quick, check there's no one inside, and we can drag him in there,' said Willow, who peeped in.

'Empty,' she said, and they dragged Sometimes by his feet inside.

Once they had set him down Willow looked around.

202

There was just one fold-up table, with a few glass bottles and vials that shimmered with strange liquid. In the corner was a large rusty wheelbarrow overflowing with goods that still needed to be unpacked.

Willow's eyes widened. 'Those look like potions,' she whispered, her eye falling on the wheelbarrow, which looked horribly familiar. Her stomach filled with dread. 'Oh no. I think we're in Amora Spell's tent. We met her in Ditchwater. Didn't go well. Just my luck we bump into her here . . .!'

'That old hag?' said Essential, eyeing the bottles in some surprise. 'I heard she was a bit of a fraud . . .'

'Me too. My grandmother was good at potions and said Amora hadn't a drop of real magic, but these, well, they look like the real thing actually . . .' Willow's eyes were drawn to the vials.

'That's because they are,' said a voice that was on the verge of a good cackle.

Willow and Essential whirled round.

'Well, dearie, we meet again,' said the hag, taking a bottle off the table and leering at them, then stepping forward menacingly. Her dark eyes snapped fire.

Nolin Sometimes's white misty eyes fluttered open and he sat up and said, 'Florence Moss.'

Willow frowned. That was her grandmother's name.

The hag looked at him, then at Willow. 'This again? What about that crazy old coot?'

'You stole these from her, before you caused the accident in the mountains of Nach,' Sometimes blurted out.

The hag's brows shot up. 'What did you say? You accuse me? I've never stolen anything in me life . . . Flossy Mossy stole from me!'

Oswin's orange head shot out of the bag. His orb-like eyes blazed with anger. '**Lies,**' he hissed.

Amora scoffed. 'She was terrible at potions, always has been, that's why she went mad . . . She was such a failure.'

'She was never a failure!' shouted Willow.

The ends of Oswin's fur started to smoke. Oswin really hated it when people lied, and he could detect lies better than most – part of his monstery kobold heritage.

Willow looked from Amora to Oswin and Sometimes, realisation dawning. 'You made it look like an accident, didn't you? You were jealous of her . . .'

'I don't know what you're talking about,' said the hag, taking a step backwards quickly. Her hands grabbed a bottle, which she threw at them.

Willow and Sometimes ducked, but nothing happened.

'I'd move quickly,' said Essential, who'd frozen the bottle and its liquid. They jumped as the bottle flew at them, and it narrowly missed its target, ricocheting off Willow's elbow and hitting Amora straight in the chest. She fell over, completely stunned, knocking over an entire shelf full of bottles in the process. There were puffs of pink and green and yellow fog that smelt of salt and lavender and cooking sherry — some of Granny Flossy's favourite things.

When the smoke cleared Sometimes checked that the hag was still breathing. 'She's been knocked out – hit by her own stolen potion.'

Willow hesitated. Part of her wanted to stay and wait for Amora to wake up so that she could get a confession out of her and clear her granny's name. But Sometimes put a hand on her shoulder.

'We've got to keep moving. I'm sorry.'

She closed her eyes, breathing deeply, and then nodded. Sometimes was right. But if she ever got her hands on Amora Spell again . . . Well, she didn't know what she'd do.

Her granny had never been the same after the accident. But Willow's father had told her that she hadn't always been like that. There had been a time when she was one of the best potion-makers in all of Starfell, when she was respected, even a bit feared. It was she, after all, who'd invented 'potion throws' – potions that didn't need to be swallowed but could be thrown at people to produce the result you wanted. Granny said it saved a lot of time trying to trick people to drink things. But after her accident many of the potions she brewed didn't go quite to plan. Now Willow knew the truth, she thought it wasn't fair that

Granny Flossy had been blamed for that accident. And it certainly wasn't fair that her career had ended because of someone's jealousy and spite.

Willow looked around Amora Spell's shelves now. There were only three bottles left, and she was loathe to leave them behind. 'These belonged to my grandmother; we should take them, and they might help—' She drew a breath. 'Granny Flossy wouldn't want her to have them anyway.' For a moment the purple hat swam before her eyes, and she felt the fear that she'd pushed down in a corner of her heart, black-tinged and pointed, the fear that something may have happened to her. Willow swallowed. Where *was* Granny Flossy?

Shaking the fear from her heart, Willow opened her bag and handed the potions labelled 'Forget', 'Wait' and 'Sleep' to Oswin, who put them next to the dragon egg, giving her hand a sympathetic pat with his green paw. Sometimes a real friend knows what to say without speaking a word. Her eyes smarted, but she drew courage from him.

# 15

## Wait and Forget

William's mother was putting away the cards and placing the crystal ball back into its velvet-lined box when Willow, Essential and Sometimes entered the caravan. Willow was determined this time to convince her mother they needed her help. But when Raine looked up she sighed, her emerald-green eyes incredulous.

'Oh, not again!'

The sentiment was echoed by Willow's sisters, who entered hot on their heels.

Camille snorted. 'Ooh, you're going to be in so much trouble!'

'Yes. Big trouble,' said Raine. 'How did you—' She stopped then, seeing Essential, and shook her head. 'So that's how you got out? Essential, I'm shocked at you. Rubix entrusted you to look after

my wayward daughter and yet here you are. I suppose she fed you the same sorry tale, and you believed it?'

'I-I'm sorry, but yes, I do,' stammered Essential, pushing up her glasses on her button nose.

Willow gave her a grateful look, then sighed. 'Look, Mum, I'm sorry, but you are wasting time and we need your help—'

Her mother spluttered in shock. 'I don't know what has come over you, Willow. When we get home your father and I will—'

But they didn't get to find out what Raine Moss planned to do as Nolin Sometimes interrupted. 'Where does Moreg Vaine live?'

Raine's eyes snapped to Sometimes, and then did a triple blink, as if this was the first time she'd noticed he was there.

But, before her mother could demand that he explain himself, Sometimes keeled over with a loud crash.

'What on Great Starfell?'

'He's all right. He's a forgotten teller – he can see the past, and that sometimes makes him faint—'

'I do *not* faint.'

They all turned to look at Sometimes, but his eyes were still cloudy. 'Parsnip Lane, Troll Country,' he murmured.

'What?' said Willow with a frown.

Sometimes turned his misty eyes on her mother. 'So you dye it? Really?'

'What?' said Raine, lifting a bejewelled hand to pat at her hair nervously.

'Light brown is a perfectly acceptable hair colour . . .'

Raine's eyes bulged. Her mouth flapped open. 'I have no idea what you're talking about . . .'

Camille let out a squeak. 'You dye your hair, Mum?'

Sometimes sat up, then cocked his head to the side with a small grin. 'So, this is Camille, eh?'

The humour died on Camille's lips and her green eyes flared. 'What's that supposed to mean?'

He shook his head. 'Oh, nothing, but it's handy having your sort of skill around when people want to hear from their dead relatives, isn't it? I mean, all you have to do is lift the rock outside with your mind and bang it against the door to make people believe that their dead have come knocking . . . Quite a clever trick.'

210

Camille had gone pale. **'W-what?'** she gasped, and then looked at her mother. 'How does he know that?'

Her mother turned to Willow, her expression somewhat embarrassed. 'It's not what you think . . .' Then she glared at Sometimes.

Willow blinked. Her mother was *a fraud*?

While her family were shouting, Sometimes looked up at her mother. 'Parsnip Lane, in Troll Country . . .' he repeated. 'I'm right?'

Raine's face blanched. 'How did you know that?'

'What?' asked Willow, thoroughly confused.

'It's where Moreg's house is.'

Willow and Essential shared a look. Troll Country?

Raine's eyes grew dark, her brow furrowed. 'I will not support this madness any longer. I'm taking you home right now . . .'

Essential leant towards Willow and whispered, 'The potions, use the potions.'

Then she raised her hands to freeze Willow's family. Willow opened the bag, took the bottles labelled 'Wait' and 'Forget', and threw them at the ground by her mother and sisters' frozen feet.

From outside came a loud crash that blew a cloud of dust into the caravan, making them stagger. Willow could hear bloodcurdling screams and what sounded like a stampede from people running helter-skelter through the market.

'What is that?' she asked.

Sometimes peered outside, then grinned. 'Feathering.'

Willow followed, seeing that the giant blue dragon was indeed roaming the grass just outside the string of tents, where he was peering inside and calling their names.

'Sorry to disturb . . . Don't wish to make a fuss. I'm just looking for my friends. You see, they've taken a bit of a long time and we really do need to press on . . . No need to scream. I am a cloud dragon, you know . . .'

'Feathering, we're here!' shouted Willow. 'Won't be a moment.'

Willow turned back to look at her family, who were oddly calm, due to the potions that had made them wait and forget. She swallowed. 'I'm sorry – um, please wait until we've left on the dragon, and then forget that I was ever here – or that you saw any of us tonight,' she said. She felt a deep pang of regret seeing them all frozen like that – especially her

mother, whose green eyes seemed to be boring into her own – but she couldn't go back home, not now they were so close to finding Moreg. And Moreg was relying on Willow; she couldn't let her down.

'Maybe I should have waited for you in the valley,' said Feathering, giving her a repentant look as a terrified couple ran past screaming blue murder.

Willow grinned. 'Your timing was excellent,' she said. 'We've just found out where Moreg's house is – it's in Troll Country.'

'Troll Country?' said Feathering, looking taken aback. 'Oh no.'

'What?'

'Well, they smell awful.'

Nolin Sometimes climbed aboard the dragon. 'They're also rather deadly with a club,' he said.

'Well, hopefully we can just get in and out as quickly as possible,' said Willow, climbing on after Sometimes and clutching her carpetbag containing Oswin.

'Come on,' said Willow to Essential, who was staring up at the dragon with enormous magnified eyes. Willow could see her swallow. 'Oh yes, sorry, you haven't yet met. This is Feathering,' Willow told Essential. 'Feathering, this is Essential Jones – she helped us escape.'

Essential stood frozen, her mouth open slightly as she took in Feathering's enormous size. There was a blub-blub sound from her lips.

'Come on, he won't bite,' said Willow, holding out a hand and helping Essential climb on to the dragon's sleek feathery back.

'Not something your size anyway,' agreed the dragon, taking a running leap and then launching off into the air, 'More of a gulp really.'

Essential gasped.

Willow shook her head. 'Now, Feathering, it's comments like that that make humans afraid of dragons.'

There was the sound of tinkly wind-chime chuckling as he beat his wings and took off into the starry sky.

At that very moment, in a dungeon beneath a fortress, a boy laughed as he threatened to kill the witch who stood before him. The potion in his hands was swirling as black as night, as black as death.

'It's just you and me now – no one else to interfere. You aren't so powerful now you're alone.'

'You're wrong,' she whispered.

'How's that?' said the boy. He flung the potion at her, and it erupted into a spray of dark, swirling fog – a fog that she couldn't escape even though she tried.

She gasped, struggling for breath. 'She will come.'

'Who – that child that was with you? You think that somehow she will save you – from this?'

Moreg closed her eyes as the smoky vapour entered her veins, and the boy's triumphant grin faltered as death didn't come. Not for her. He should have known that she would fight, that she would be able to cling on to life long after anyone else would have given up.

## 16

## Calamity Troll

Troll Country lay in a somewhat dented and bruised corner of Starfell few dared visit. Not surprising when its inhabitants saw carrying a weapon studded with nails and spikes as part of their national identity. It certainly wasn't your top choice for a holiday destination.

In fact, very few people aside from trolls ventured to Troll Country unless they were rather desperate, or very stupid, or, like Willow and her friends, desperate but also in the company of a *dragon*. Even if he wasn't really the dangerous sort, the trolls wouldn't know *that*, or so Willow hoped.

The journey to Troll Country was a long one, and they'd managed to get a few hours' sleep on Feathering's back. Nolin Sometimes had worried that it would be dangerous to sleep in case they fell off,

unless they had a bit of rope. Of course no one had, but Essential had mentioned that she'd once lost an old skipping rope, which was rather lucky. A few seconds later, it had come hurtling across the sky into Willow's outstretched hands, and they'd managed to strap themselves securely to Feathering.

In the morning their stomachs started to grumble with hunger. Oswin passed around a loaf of bread and cheese he'd pilfered from the caravan when no one was looking. **'Wot?'** he said innocently, scratching behind his ear with a rusty claw. **'I knows we're saving the world and everyfing, but body's got to eat, don't it?'**

Just before noon, they arrived at a barren wasteland of rocky hills and bleached sand. Any plants or grassland had long been flattened beneath large flat feet and the landscape looked dented, like holey cheese. Feathering explained that this was a result of the trolls' daily club-throwing contests. As they flew they saw tented villages and trolls of all kinds walking about dragging their knuckles, and their clubs, on the ground. Luckily none of them looked upwards and spotted Feathering and his passengers.

Even from high in the sky Willow could safely say, based on the smell alone, that these were the sorts of creatures who might benefit from a large deal of soap and water. They made Oswin smell like a rose bush, which was saying something.

Following Sometimes's directions, Feathering landed on a hillside.

'From what I saw of your mother's memories there's a cave somewhere close by,' said Sometimes, slipping off Feathering's back, 'and from there, once you get inside, you'll exit into a little valley leading to Parsnip Lane.'

'Why would she choose to live here?' asked Essential, pushing her glasses up on her small nose, which wrinkled in puzzlement.

'I have no idea,' said Sometimes, his eyes wide.

'It certainly can't be for the peace and quiet,' said Feathering as the distant sounds of clubs and fists rumbled the hillside.

'Or the smell of the country air,' agreed Willow, stuffing her sister's horseshoe scarf under her nose as they made their way inside a damp, mouldy cave, which was just wide enough for Feathering. As they entered they heard a dripping sound followed by

219

something that sounded like a waterfall. A waterfall, however, that was sniffling every few seconds.

Willow's eyes adjusted to the gloom. On the ground were the littered remains of bleached bones, and as she stepped further into the cave she heard the sniffling sound again. 'Did you hear that?' she asked.

The others shook their heads.

From within the bag she could hear a faint '*Oh no . . . Oh, me greedy aunt . . .*'

She swallowed. That was never a good sign.

Willow heard the sniffling again and paused. 'This way,' she said, beckoning, and led her friends deeper into the cave. Up ahead they could hear the sound of gushing water and in the gloom they could see large stalagmites and stalactites.

From one of his many pockets Nolin Sometimes produced a small lantern, and Feathering obliged by puffing a tiny bit of fire into it. Through the flames they saw that they were not alone after all.

Someone was crying. A rather big someone who looked to be made of stone, except for the part of it that had very red hair in two long plaits down its back.

They approached very cautiously.

'Are you all right?' asked Willow, kneeling beside what looked a bit like an enormous stone ear the size of a small dinner plate.

The figure snuffled and turned a very large, very wide face towards Willow; it was marked by two long tracks of tears. It blinked enormous green eyes that were filled with water, which spilled over and splashed Willow's shoes.

'I-I thought I was alone up here,' said the stone-like figure.

'Is that why you were crying?' asked Willow, realising that it wasn't a person made of stone; it was a *troll*. She'd never seen one up close before. In fact, the only time she'd ever seen one was on a **'Beware of the Troll'** sign, which usually showed a big figure with wild matted red hair, sloping shoulders, missing teeth and a club. But the troll crying in front of Willow had all its teeth, very neat red hair and didn't seem to have a club. Still. It was a troll. *Definitely a troll.*

The creature shook its head. 'No . . . I was crying because, well . . . I can't remember what happened. And I can't go back until I do.'

Willow handed the troll her horseshoe scarf to mop up her tears, which the troll took gratefully in its big stony fingers, dabbing rather delicately at its eyes.

'Can't go back where?' asked Willow.

'Home,' said the troll.

'And why can't you go home?' continued Willow, jumping aside as more tears rained down.

The troll sniffed. 'Well, I was meant to fight the great Verushka.' She paused for emphasis, then stared at their blank faces. 'You know who she is?'

The friends shook their heads. This seemed to stop the troll's crying temporarily at least.

'Well, Verushka is the greatest warrior in all the troll tribes.'

**'Wot, and yew were meant to fight this warrior?'** blurted Oswin, who was eyeing the proceedings as usual from a hole in the hairy bag. At the troll's look the bag started to shake a little. **'It's jes, I means, *well . . .'***

The troll sniffed, then hung her head. 'No, you're right. I don't look like a warrior, do I?' she said. Willow noted her neat hair and rather clean and fresh scent, like limestone, and couldn't help nodding in agreement.

'Well, surely that's not the end of the world?' asked Willow.

The troll shook her head. 'You see, you may not know this, but most trolls aren't very sensitive.'

'Really?' said Willow, giving the bag a small shake as the kobold started to giggle.

The troll continued. 'Well, in my family "Fierce" is the family motto. All my brothers have necklaces made out of human bones that spell F-E-E-R-S.' The troll gave a woeful smile. 'They aren't good spellers either,' she said with a grin.

'My father was the chief, my mother was his general,

but that was before she defeated him and made him her slave,' she said with a bit of a nostalgic sigh.

At their shocked expressions she shook her head. 'Oh, that's normal in troll marriages. She built him a cage that she keeps right under her throne, which is also built out of bones. It's something of a theme, bones. She lets him out every few months when she's feeling a little sentimental . . .'

At their gasps she continued. 'That's considered quite a healthy troll relationship. Most troll wives eat their mates when they get too disagreeable, generally sometime within the first year of marriage . . . See, troll females are often the strongest and most vicious. They're quite a lot bigger and hairier than the males, so they are much more valued. Well, usually. I'm the only girl in my family. As the chief's daughter I was the pride of the clan . . . until I became their biggest calamity . . . which is funny, really, because that's actually my name,' she said with a deep sigh.

'Anyway, my mother tried her best, but I just didn't take to being a troll. Trolls live by the maxim, "*Club everything that moves once and club things that don't twice.*" Only, of course, I didn't like clubbing things. I was meant to go out every day and learn how to use

my club. Which seemed like a monumental waste of time. You pick it up, you conk somebody – it's not hard to grasp.' She sighed.

Suddenly Sometimes keeled over backwards in a dead faint.

'Oh no, not again!' cried Essential and Willow at the same time.

'What's happened?' asked the troll, peering into the gloom.

But before Willow could explain properly Sometimes sat up, his eyes white. 'You used to hide away from your family pretending that you were practising the club but you actually went to the woods beyond this cave, where you kept a garden no one knew about . . . and had a rabbit,' he whispered.

The troll's eyes widened, and she gasped. 'How does he know that?'

'He sees the past,' explained Willow.

The troll looked away, her face twisted in shame. She nodded. 'He's right. I did. He wasn't even, you know, for food . . . I just liked him. I even gave him a name. But when my mother found out it was the worst day of my life,' she said, hanging her head.

225

'Trolls don't have pets?' guessed Essential, pushing up her glasses.

Calamity frowned. 'Well, no. I mean, I suppose Dad is a kind of pet . . . but no troll has ever kept a pet rabbit before or grown daisies just because they were pretty. But my mother . . . she did try to understand in her way, after she sent my brothers to destroy the garden . . . and Jawbone.'

'Jawbone?' asked Feathering.

'The rabbit.'

Feathering gasped. 'The beasts!'

Calamity nodded. 'He ran away thankfully. But that's when the crying started, because I thought they'd killed him at first. The crying was the last straw, my mother said. I didn't know what was happening to me; no one else did either. They had to send for the dwarf from across the valley. Dwarfs are wise, you know. Anyway, he explained that crying was something that *humans* did.' She looked mortified.

'Don't trolls cry?' asked Sometimes.

'No,' said Calamity. 'Well, you can just imagine my family's reaction. My brothers wanted to build me my own cage . . . right next to Dad's. But my mother decided to give me one last chance. She's a thinker,

my mother – rare in trolls – but I think she knew that unless I sorted myself out I'd forever be a scar against her name. So, under my own mother's guidance, my training began. It was horrid,' she said with a shudder.

'But finally she said I was about as ready as I ever would be and last Tuesday I was meant to fight the great Verushka. But I don't remember it.'

'You don't remember anything?'

She shook her head. 'And neither does anyone else, which some people thought was a bit suspicious. There were some who thought that maybe I had other human traits that I'd used.'

'Human traits? Like what?' asked Willow.

'Like magic – and maybe I'd made them forget somehow. I saw my brothers working on a cage in secret. So while they were sleeping I ran away, but I still can't remember what happened and until I do I can't go home. So I'm stuck, perhaps forever.'

Willow shook her head. 'I don't think so.'

At Calamity's look of surprise Willow told her what had happened to the missing Tuesday.

'So that's what happened to me? The day was taken and with it my memories?' asked Calamity, her eyes wide.

Feathering nodded. 'We think so,' he said, telling her about the baby dragon that should have hatched.

The troll's eyes filled with tears. 'Oh, I'm so sorry.'

'It's happened to all of us,' said Willow, swallowing as the purple hat with its jaunty feather – Granny Flossy's hat – swam before her eyes, her face turned away from her. 'And I think the thing I can't remember from the missing day has something to do with my grandmother . . . Maybe . . . something bad.'

Essential touched her shoulder. 'It might not be.'

'We have to find out what happened,' said Willow, squaring her shoulders. 'Even if –' her eyes filled – 'even if maybe I'd rather not know . . .'

Calamity sniffed, then nodded. 'You're right. It's better to know. I might have been defeated. I probably was – but at least I would have proven that I was a troll, even if I was beaten. So how are you going to find the missing Tuesday?'

Willow explained about their plan and how they needed to find Moreg's house.

'It's on Parnsip Lane,' she explained.

The troll nodded. 'I know the way – I'll show you,' she said, standing up and making the cave shudder. Willow blinked as the young troll towered over them

228

at a massive eleven feet. Seeing their looks of surprise, Calamity shrugged, so that a neat red plait fell over her shoulder. 'Yup, shortest troll you ever saw? I get that a lot,' she said with a woeful smile that was even more surprising for its row of perfect white teeth.

Willow shook her head. Calamity was the *only* troll she'd ever seen.

As they exited the cave into the valley beyond Willow couldn't help thinking that they were the oddest ragtag group of creatures ever seen. From the pearly indigo-blue dragon, Feathering, to the stony troll, Calamity, short Essential Jones, skinny Nolin Sometimes, herself, and her monster, Oswin. And for about a second, as she stepped into the warm sunshine, she felt a sense of pride at the small army she had assembled to rescue Moreg and the lost day.

Well, until she saw the storm of trolls waiting for them on the other side.

From within the hairy carpetbag came a small gasp. '***Oh no.***'

# 17

## The Troll Army

There must have been close to twenty trolls, though it felt like more as each one of them was over fifteen feet high, stinking to high heaven and wearing what looked like bits of human bone and teeth like odd, misshapen jewellery.

Willow took an involuntarily step backwards as the biggest and hairiest troll was carried forward on a large throne made of bones. This troll was wearing what looked like an old vest and a leather skirt, her grey stone-like body covered in lichen, and when she opened her mouth she gave a pitying sort of grin, full of lots of mossy teeth. '*Humans*, Calamity? What have we told you about playing with your food?'

Calamity bit her lip. 'Um, Mum, I can explain.'

The troll chief sighed in a way that Willow

recognised – she'd seen the same sort of look on her mother's face enough times in the past.

'Really? We've been looking for you . . . It's not very *troll* to run away.'

The trolls around her started cracking their knuckles and pounding their clubs on the ground in agreement.

'I told them you were young, scared, not ready yet for your destiny, afraid to follow in your father's noble footsteps,' she said, pointing to a giant cage beneath the throne in which a smaller troll was squashed. He raised three stony fingers to wave woefully at his daughter.

'But I never thought it was true . . . that you had really gone to the witch beyond the cave for help. Except, here you are.'

Calamity twiddled her long red plait nervously. 'It's not like that,' she told the ground.

Willow stepped forward. 'It's the witch who needs *your* help.'

The troll chief blinked enormous moss-coloured eyes. 'Did that little ant just speak to me?' she asked in shock. There were guffaws all around.

Feathering took a step forward, his head lowering

menacingly. Golden eyes gleaming.

'Oh, I see the humans brought along a pet,' she said. 'Kind of you to consider us like that – a bunch of skinny humans doesn't really go too far for dinner. This, however, should do nicely,' she said, eyeing Feathering's considerable size.

He snarled, smoke curling out of his nostrils.

'**Seize them,**' said the troll chief.

A nearby troll grabbed Willow and lifted her up. Willow's mind whirred and then she did something that was rather brave and rather stupid.

'**Verushka!**' she shouted.

Everyone around her gasped. 'She dares to speak the name of our greatest warrior! Did she just call the great Verushka by her name?'

Suddenly an enormous thirteen-foot troll powered to the front. Her skin was like granite, her red hair a collection of knotty coils like serpent's tails, and her anthracite eyes glinted with cold fire.

Willow swallowed. 'You want to know what happened last Tuesday, right? What happened at the battle?'

'I KNOW WHAT HAPPENED!' she roared.

Willow shook her head, swallowed, then summoned up all her courage and the air in her lungs and shouted,

## 'NO, YOU *DON'T* AND NEITHER DOES ANYONE ELSE!'

There was a deafening silence all around, then the trolls started to murmur among themselves.

The troll holding her squeezed her painfully round the middle. 'Squelch it? Can I squelch it?'

There were murmurs of agreement all round.

'Dimsrat likes to squash,' said the troll, referring to herself in the third person. 'Best squasher.'

As the troll shook her the hairy carpetbag opened and some of the contents came crashing down, including the last of Granny Flossy's potions: 'Sleep'. Oswin shot out a green shaggy paw to save it, then threw it at Dimsrat, who keeled over, releasing Willow as she did, and erupted into loud snores.

There were several gasps from the trolls. They were clearly terrified of magic.

Willow whispered her thanks to Oswin, then picked up the bag. The trolls stepped back. She frowned. They didn't know that was her last potion. She took courage from that.

'Verushka,' she said again. This time no one protested that she dared to speak her name. The illusion of magic had given her respect, and she relied

upon that now as she needed them to hear her out.

'We know you *probably* did defeat Calamity, of course; look at you, how could it be otherwise?'

The air was full of loud catcalls and the sound of fists bumping into each other, and clubs scraping along the ground.

'*And yet . . .*' whispered Willow, and every single one of them stopped.

'Yet,' she continued, filling the silence, 'there she stands with not even a scratch. How is that possible?'

'BECAUSE WE NEVER FOUGHT. SHE'D BE DEAD OTHERWISE!' thundered Verushka, pounding her chest with a boulder-like fist.

Willow shrugged. 'Can you be sure of that? Can they?'

Verushka roared. 'ENOUGH OF THIS – I'M GOING TO SQUASH YOU MYSELF. I DON'T CARE WHAT MAGIC YOU HAVE!'

'You could – but that won't change the fact that you will never know if you really *did* defeat her. But I know how we can find out.'

The troll chief looked at Willow, narrowing her eyes. 'You know what happened?'

She shook her head. 'No, but—'

There were shouts all round. 'Finish her! Squelch! Squelch!'

'But I know why none of us know what happened!' shouted Willow.

'What do you mean?' asked Verushka, who'd finally stopped hollering.

'Last Tuesday has gone missing – and with it all of our memories of what happened on that day, including what happened between you and Calamity on the battlefield. The day was taken away using a spell.'

'Magic! I knew it was magic!' cried Verushka.

Many of the other trolls nodded as well. One of them seized Calamity. 'It was you! You who do things like the humans!'

'She had nothing to do with it. It was a spell that was used by a Brother of Wol.'

'The little humans who wear brown sheets and have tried to create laws that forbid us from coming near them?' asked the troll chief.

Willow nodded. She was grateful that the Brothers' interfering reputation had even reached Troll Country.

'The witch who lives in the valley has asked for my help to find the spell and to restore the missing day.'

237

'Your help – why yours?'

'Because that's what I do – I find things that are lost.'

'And if you find this spell, then we will all remember what happened? If we fought or that I won?' asked Versuska.

Willow nodded.

There were mutterings all around. Trolls didn't feel fear . . . except when it came to magic. Magic wasn't something you could beat down with brute strength; it couldn't be put in a cage or told to feel inferior because of its size – and for trolls that was something they couldn't understand.

The troll chief looked like she was trying to make up her mind. Even Verushka hesitated.

'I'll go,' said Calamity. 'I will go with them and help them to bring back the day.'

There were gasps.

'Mama Chief, I know I'm not your idea of what a troll should be. And if we do remember what happened, I'm fairly sure it will be that I was defeated. But I can do this – I can help,' she said, swallowing nervously.

There were a few relieved-looking trolls. None of them were that keen on being close to magic. The troll chief nodded. 'Very well.'

'But,' said Willow, thinking fast, 'if she succeeds, if we all succeed in restoring last Tuesday and our memories, I think Calamity deserves a new deal. There will be no cages in her future . . . She can just be accepted for who she is.'

Calamity's mother was silent for a very long time and then she said, 'All right.'

Willow added quickly, 'And, um, I think you should unlock her father as well.'

**'Ooh, don' push it,'** whispered Oswin from inside the bag.

'He'll come out when he admits that he should have asked for directions to the troll gathering twelve moons ago.'

'Never,' said Calamity's father.

The troll chief shrugged. 'Suit yourself.'

Then she took off a long leather necklace from which hung an odd-shaped bone whistle.

'I'm putting my trust in Calamity – but if you need us, just blow on this.'

Which is how, to Willow's complete shock and amazement, she found herself in possession of a whistle that would summon an entire troll army.

# 18

## The Witch's House

'How on earth are we going to fit a troll and a dragon through that?' said Nolin Sometimes, pointing up ahead at a tiny ramshackle stone hut that was nestled deep in the valley.

'I have no idea,' said Willow, eyes widening as they approached it. The house was minuscule with just one window and a weather-beaten door, which was hanging ajar.

'It's hard to imagine Moreg Vaine living here,' said Essential with a puzzled frown.

Willow couldn't help but agree. She thought of the witch's statement about her 'other cellar', which had made her think that Moreg's home was rather large, not the tiny hut they stood in front of now.

Willow tried opening the front door, but it was locked.

Sometimes tried the window, but that wouldn't budge either.

'We may need to break it,' concluded Essential.

There was a faint shaking from the bag and she could hear Oswin's wails of **'Oh *no!* Oh, me greedy aunt! Osbertrude!'** growing louder. She frowned, he usually only got this worked up about the curse of his aunt if there was intense magic around.

Willow picked up a rock and threw it at the window but it barely made a scratch, and even when Calamity tried putting her sizable fist through the glass and then tried kicking the door down with one of her boulder-like feet nothing happened.

Willow took out the StoryPass, which was whirring round as if in confusion. 'Oswin's on to something; I think this has been charmed somehow.'

Essential's eyes widened, and she fished out the hag stone and peered through the hole. 'Yes, oh my goodness, you'll never believe it!' she exclaimed.

'What is it?' asked Willow.

Essential handed her the stone so that Willow could see for herself.

She peered through the small hole in the stone and gasped.

It was a golden castle with marble turrets and spires winking high in the sky. Instead of the half-broken doorway they were standing in front of enormous polished doors that were over fifteen feet high – high enough for even the tallest troll to pass through.

Willow passed the stone around for Sometimes, Feathering, Calamity and Oswin to see – even the kobold was impressed before he zipped himself back inside the bag for safety.

Holding the stone, Willow tried the door, which swung open at once, with a loud deafening clatter. Oswin was right – the hag stone worked when you were outside the charm!

'Come on,' she said, walking through a long passageway.

On the walls were paintings of curious objects and plants. Nolin Sometimes paused before one of a jam jar with a odd purple flower shaped a bit like a house, and frowned. 'Oooh, I didn't know she was into magical botany . . . I suppose it is Moreg . . .'

In the corners of the passage were statues, or what looked at first like statues, except that they seemed to be sleeping . . .

'Oh!' exclaimed Essential eyeing them warily. 'These are enchanted stone figures! Rubix's specialty. It's best we get away from them . . . I had to fight one when I was little. Rubix thought it was good practice . . .'

'And was it?' asked Willow.

'For getting some impressive bruises – very.'

They shared a grin.

There was a small passageway to the left that led to a set of stone stairs. Willow stopped. 'Maybe we should go this way . . .'

They all nodded. As curious as Willow was to see the rest of the castle they needed to get to the kitchen. 'Come on, we need to find the pantry to get to Moreg.'

The others followed her down the stairs, which led to a basement kitchen. They raced inside, passing a massive wooden table and an old forest-green range.

Through a separate door to the side they found the enormous pantry. 'Here,' Willow said as they entered.

It was filled with dozens of shelves and on either side were steps that Willow guessed must lead to a set of cellars. 'It'll be one of these,' said Willow, guessing aloud. 'Our first night away, while we were camping, she said she'd left something in her other cellar . . . which means the portal must only work on one side,' she concluded.

They were about to turn and look at the other cellar when she saw something she recognised.

'Hang on,' said Willow seeing a fold-up chair, along with an iron pot, a table and two broomsticks –

including Whisper! 'It must be around here somewhere,' she said. She placed her hands against the wall, feeling all along the surface. It had to be here – it had to! Then suddenly her fingers pressed straight through the stone until she was touching something soft and silken – like the lining inside a cloak. 'It's here!' She shot her friends a nervous look and said, 'I'll go first.'

Sometimes looked a little anxious himself. 'We'll be right behind you,' he reassured her.

Willow took a deep breath, picked up the bag with Oswin inside and then pushed her way through the wall and the fabric.

She found herself tumbling
down until she landed in a heap on
a stone floor in a dark and dusty
room, Oswin protesting loudly.

'Keep it down,' Willow
hissed, rubbing her head.
She glanced up and saw
that the cloak had been
hanging from a hook
above her.

But where was
Moreg?

Willow stood up,
just as Sometimes
fell through the
cloak, followed
closely by
Essential, who
landed on top
of him, her
glasses askew.
'Ouch!' they both
muttered.

Disentangling himself, Sometimes crossed the room and made a funny noise. Soon Willow and Essential could see why. On the floor one of the Brothers was sprawled on to his back, a purplish lump on his forehead.

'Knocked out,' confirmed Sometimes, his eyes going glassy and rolling back as the memory washed over him. A moment later, while his eyes were clouded and white, he continued. 'He's a prison guard. They locked Moreg up here in this dungeon, and she waited until he came inside, then she hit him over the head with a pot from her pantry and stole his keys. The last thing the guard saw before he passed out was that she left her cloak on the peg. She must have done that so that we'd be able to find her,' he said, just as a giant troll foot was making its way out of the cloak's folds.

'Rather clever,' came a voice from behind them, accompanied by a smattering of mocking applause.

'**Oh no,**' moaned Oswin.

Willow spun round to find that several Brothers of Wol, including the High Master, were making their way into the room.

'Oh dear,' said Sometimes, falling over into a dead faint.

# 19

## Magic in Wolkana

A group of priests crowded into the cell and a spotty-faced Brother, who looked vaguely familiar, stepped forward. 'Burn it,' he commanded.

'What?' said the High Master with a puzzled frown as one of the Brothers seized a candle that was hanging in a sconce on the wall and flung it at the cloak. It set alight instantly.

'Stop!' shouted Willow.

Essential raised her hands and they watched as the flames paused for almost a full second, long enough for them to see the massive troll foot disappear back, followed by Feathering's golden eye, which had been peering at them from within the folds of the cloak.

Willow sagged in relief, glad that Calamity and Feathering had retreated to safety before the cloak

went up in flames. But relief was replaced with despair as she watched their only means of escape go up in smoke.

'We can't have you using that again,' said the Brother, seeming to sense her thoughts.

Looking at him properly, Willow recognised him as the one who'd run away from her and Moreg to fetch the High Master in Beady Hill.

'See here, missy,' said the High Master now, his black pebble-like eyes wide. 'I'm not sure what your business is. If you think that you've come to kidnap our . . .' He looked around, his face going slack in surprise when he saw the guard on the floor. 'What on Great Starfell?! What's happened? Where is Moreg Vaine? What have you done with her?' he demanded of Willow. The High Master's eyes trailed to the charred remains of the cloak. 'Did she escape? Did you see what happened?'

The young Brother came forward and placed a hand on the High Master's shoulder. 'There's nothing to worry about; it's all been taken care of – the witch has been moved . . .'

'Moved?' said the High Master, blinking. Willow could see the confusion in his small, dark eyes.

249

'What is going on here? What is this?' he asked.

'Nothing for you to worry about,' soothed the Brother, patting the High Master's shoulder. 'Easily explained . . .'

The High Master blinked, his eye falling on Sometimes, who was still lying passed out on the floor alongside the knocked-out guard. 'But *why* was she moved? Why wasn't I told?'

Nolin Sometimes's eyes were large and glassy and a faint whisper escaped his lips, '*The boy . . . the boy used the spell for his second attempt to seize the post of High Master.*'

'What?' gasped the High Master. '*What* did he just say?'

'*The boy used the spell for his second attempt to seize the post of High Master,*' Sometimes repeated before his eyes closed and he fell back into a dead faint.

The High Master bent down and tried to wake up Sometimes, but he was out for the count. 'Ludicrous, why would someone say such a thing . . .? A spell? Magic in Wolkana? What nonsense. Seizing power? I *am* the High Master. No one would try such a thing. I think this man might be unwell.'

The younger spotty-faced Brother nodded. 'Yes, that must be it. Quite unwell. I think perhaps you should take him to the infirmary, and then we can deal with these, er, children, and their friends with their peculiar tales when you return.' Two Brothers stepped forward to pick up Nolin Sometimes, and the High Master nodded. 'Yes, maybe that's best, Silas,' he said, turning to go with them.

Willow tensed. *Silas?* The words from the memory flower reverberated inside her skull. *The boy called Silas cast the spell hidden within the fortress.*

She gasped, then looked at Sometimes, who was still unconscious.

'Wait,' said Willow, her mind working fast. 'He's a forgotten teller – one who sees the past – and he saw that a boy – Silas – used a spell that stole last Tuesday, a spell that could end up destroying the world if we don't fix it. You have to help us, please.'

The High Master scoffed. 'What nonsense. Silas seize power? Magic here, in Wolkana? We have tried for centuries to rid Starfell of this filth, this evil from the world. We would never allow it here . . . *never.*'

It was just a second but Willow saw the anger on

the young Brother Silas's face. 'No, that's true. *You* wouldn't,' he sneered.

The High Master looked at him with a frown.

From Nolin Sometimes's prone form they heard him mutter. '*The Lost Spells of Starfell were kept out of sight for a thousand years in a gilded box, hidden in the fortress, until the boy named Silas found them and sought to use them for himself . . .*'

The High Master turned ashen. He seemed to stagger slightly. His mouth fell open and he looked at Silas, blinking. 'I-it can't be true? What they are saying . . . You wouldn't have . . . you couldn't have found them, and actually *used* them?' His hand was on his heart. Willow could tell that he was finding it hard to breathe.

Silas scowled. He looked at Willow and Nolin Sometimes, who had passed out again, with something close to a mix of frustration and amusement. 'You just *had* to bring a forgotten teller along.'

Willow frowned. 'What?'

He sighed. 'I had hoped for a bit more time . . . or at least preferable surroundings,' he said, eyeing the dungeon in some distaste. A few of the other Brothers shared a knowing sort of smile with him.

Willow felt something inside her turn cold as he continued.

Silas looked at the High Master, his mouth turning up into a thin, humourless smile. 'There is no need for this pretence any more, High Master. I fear the secret is out, don't you? The truth always comes out in the end . . . no matter what lengths one goes to.' He reached inside his robes and withdrew a small box.

The High Master's face blanched as he saw what was in Silas's hands. 'W-what secret? Silas, think of what you are saying . . . and who you are speaking to,' he said, shooting a meaningful look at Willow and her friends, his eyes then straying back to the box. 'You don't want them to leave here with the wrong impression. We can't have them thinking that magic would ever be permitted in Wolkana—'

'ENOUGH!' thundered Silas. He didn't look nearly as frightened or as young as he had when they'd seen him in Beady Hill. In fact, he didn't even look all that young any more. His spots were gone, and his face was lean and hard, like the expression in his eyes.

Willow blinked. It was as if he'd used magic until

now to make himself appear less powerful. But how could that be?

His voice was cold. 'LIES. *All of them*, and I grow weary of each one. Seize him,' he ordered, and three of the Brothers stepped forward to take the High Master away.

'Silas? What is this – a rebellion?' His voice cracked. 'So it's all *true* – what they said? Silas, my boy, my child, *why*?'

'*Now* he claims me,' said Silas, gritting his teeth. 'Wol help me. But it is too late for that, *Father*, much, much too late, I'm afraid. Perhaps if you'd thought, just once, to let go of your reputation, to accept me as your son and heir . . . perhaps things would have worked out differently. But you are weak and that is something that we can no longer afford to have in a leader.'

Willow frowned. The High Master was Silas's father?

The High Master blinked. 'I-I, Silas, I thought you understood – a man in my position, I couldn't just come out publicly and say you were my son . . .'

Silas shook his head. 'No, Father, you chose to keep it a secret because you were ashamed of who my mother was.'

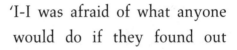

'I-I was afraid of what anyone would do if they found out . . . how it would seem. You must understand . . . It wasn't because I didn't care about you!'

'Yes, how would it seem if they all discovered that the High Master had fallen in love with a *witch* and had a child with magic running through his veins?'

Willow and Essential gasped. A Brother of Wol, the son of a *witch*?

The High Master's cheeks turned purple. He bounced on the balls of his feet and tried waving his hands as if he would scrub away Silas's words, but one of the guards held him back.

'Silas, stop this – please.'

Silas looked from the High Master to Willow and Essential. 'The High Master, of course, was the only one who knew the truth . . . about who I am. But he kept it a secret for years – even from me.'

The High Master stuttered. 'S-Silas . . . I did it for your own good. To *protect* you.'

'No,' said Silas, his eyes cold. 'You did it for your own protection, in case anyone found out that my mother, Molsa, was the sister of the infamous witch Moreg Vaine—'

'Moreg?' cried Willow.

Inside the carpetbag there was a small audible gasp.

Silas nodded. 'Yes, *Moreg*, my "loving" aunt brought me here after her sister died and left me here with him,' he said, pointing at the High Master. 'My father, though he never told anyone, of course,' he scoffed.

The High Master blinked. 'Silas, you must understand I was worried about what people would do to you if they knew—'

'Oh. I understand . . . more than you know. Remember I was raised to believe that people like me were tainted, *impure.* I came to you in the beginning when my magic arrived . . . when I was worried, afraid. But hopeful too – perhaps this meant something else. I was a Brother of Wol, after all. Surely then magic couldn't *really* be evil? And what did you tell me, when I needed you the most?'

The High Master grew pale, his mouth opening and closing.

'You told me you were disgusted, that I should rid myself of my unnaturalness . . . And you made me pray every day for Wol to take it away . . . Oh, how I cursed you when I found out the truth about who I really am – where I'd come from.'

'I wanted to help you, that's all. I—'

'Help? No, you wanted to punish me, for what you'd done. Never once did it occur to you to tell me that my mother was a witch, or to find a way to really help me. But . . . I learnt to rely on myself, and in the end, Father, you were the blind one,' Silas spat, 'so blind. And under your very roof too. Did you never wonder about any of it – how we were able to acquire these, for instance?' he said, brandishing a pair of

257

manacles that glowed blue in his hands.

'They were gifts . . . from Wol, hidden in the . . . dungeons, for centuries . . .' said the High Master, though he was sounding less sure of himself now.

Silas looked amused. 'Wrong again. I made these. You believe too much in the lies we were told. Which is what keeps *us weak*. Shying away from the truth always does. But I know the truth now, why the war began all those years ago. It was not to rid the world of magic because it was evil, but to take it back,' he breathed, '*Back to where it belongs – with us*.' His smile was great and horrible and seeing it made Willow shiver.

'No,' gasped the High Master. 'That's a lie – we were never meant to *use* the magic, never. Only to protect others from it.'

Silas looked at him, then allowed himself a small smile. 'That's what you said the first time too. You are nothing if not constant.'

'The first time? What are you talking about?'

Willow's brain was whirring as pieces of the puzzle floated around, snapping into place. 'That's why you cast the spell – it was to take away the memory, wasn't it? The memory of the day you *first* tried to seize power?'

Silas turned to her. 'Yes – very clever. That first attempt all went horribly wrong and I was thwarted. But by taking the day away I got to have another chance . . . and this time I knew I would get it right.'

He whirled to face the High Master. 'You see, Father, we've actually had this discussion before . . . though I wasn't as prepared as I am now. So it went a bit differently. It was me in chains that day once you'd found me with the spells . . .'

Silas clicked his fingers, and a Brother stepped forward to snap the manacles on to the High Master's wrists.

'Silas, no!'

'I'd been so careful, or so I thought . . . I had made sure that no one in Wolkana knew about the rebellion I was planning. Only the Brothers I trusted with my life. And I was right. No one here did know. I hadn't factored on a witch a thousand miles away, who would foresee it . . . or how she was afraid of what it would mean . . . that with these spells I could become as powerful as the last magicians of Starfell . . . so she tried to warn you by sending a raven. At first you didn't believe her . . . But then you found me with the box, and you locked up your

259

own son . . .' His eyes were dark with hatred at the memory. 'You are no father of mine. Take him,' he instructed, and the High Master was dragged away screaming.

# 20

## ✳ Enough to Make a Kobold Explode

✳

'Moreg,' breathed Willow when Silas turned to face her. 'She was the witch who saw what you were planning, wasn't she?'

Silas cocked his head to the side and seemed to almost smile. 'You are a clever witch.'

Willow shared a look with Essential. Perhaps there was a way they could still escape and find Moreg. She knew it was important to keep him talking at least.

'But how did you get the spell to take away the day – if he'd locked you up?'

'My father didn't have the heart to take me to the dungeons, not his only child. So he locked me in my room under guard. But that guard was a Brother who was faithful to me and my cause. I persuaded him to help me escape and I retrieved the spells so that I could have a second chance. But first I had to get rid

261

of the memory of my first attempt and lure Moreg here so that she couldn't thwart me a second time. And I have – and this time I will do it right. Whatever it takes.'

There was a noise from the floor. Sometimes was finally coming round. He sat up, his face as white as a sheet. 'What have you done?' he asked Silas.

'What was necessary. My father wasn't the only one who had to be stopped . . .'

Just then two Brothers came inside the cell carrying Moreg Vaine. Her body was still, her eyes closed.

'NO!' shouted Willow, racing towards her. One of the Brothers seized her by her middle.

'She's dead?' gasped Willow, feeling her stomach twist in fear and remorse.

'No – alas,' said Silas. 'Though I did try my best. She's managed to put herself into some kind of protective sleep . . . though death is what she deserves.'

'Why? Just because she told your father what you were planning? How you had taken the spells?' asked Essential.

He shook his head. 'It is more than that. *She* was the one who brought me here to Wolkana in the first place. Even when she *knew* that I would have magical

ability. How could I not – being the child of her sister? Yet she left me here anyway, knowing, perhaps better than anyone, how the Brothers and my father feel about people with magic – and how he would raise me to believe that everything about me was wrong. For that alone she deserves to suffer, but most of all for getting in my way again – and trying to thwart my plans.

'I hoped that when I cast the spell and stole last Tuesday that no one, including the great Moreg Vaine, would remember the day and its events. I knew, though, for Moreg it would be a temporary thing. Even if the spell caused her to forget the past, even if it changed the fabric of time, it couldn't stop her eventually seeing the future and working out what I had done – not with her magical abilities . . .'

Willow blinked in sudden realisation. *Of course.* Moreg, who seemed somehow able to do anything . . . 'She's a seer.' It made sense. The way Moreg seemed to plan ahead and know things – like how she would be captured, and how Willow would find an unusual garden in Nolin Sometimes's old childhood home, or that she would need to find Essential Jones . . . Willow thought back to how occasionally the witch's eyes had gone hazy,

almost the way Nolin Sometimes's eyes did . . .

She thought too of how the witch had scoffed at the sorts of people who called themselves fortune tellers and got information from the dead . . . like maybe she knew how it really worked.

'The only real seer in Starfell, I'd guess.' Silas smirked begrudgingly. 'That's why I needed something clever, something to fool a witch. The spell I chose was perfect; it hid the events of last Tuesday, so my father wouldn't remember my plans, or see them coming. But I knew that I was on borrowed time as the spell would mess with the future – a future the great Moreg Vaine would question. I knew it would most likely bring her here as a result – she wouldn't trust sending a raven to warn my father a second time, but this time I would be ready for her. It was all rather brilliant, I thought. Felling two birds with one stone.

'I didn't know about you, though – I hadn't factored on a little girl who finds – what is it? Lost things? I suppose she thought you might help her to find the missing day. Perhaps she even believed that you would be able to save her? But, alas, that is not a chance I'm willing to take, you see. I can't let you live knowing any of this.' He took a bottle from his robes, one that

shimmered with a strange dark liquid. He uncorked it and there was a smell of burnt toast and rubber.

Willow's eyes widened. Was that what she feared it was? If so, it was highly illegal. Granny had said that only those with pure evil in their souls could make it. From within the hairy carpetbag there was a very faint '*Oh no.*'

'I see you know this, child – it's the potion of death. Alas, this doesn't work as a "potion throw"; the only way for it to have a permanent effect is to swallow it. But the results are instant, so there's that to look forward to – there should be enough for all of you.'

He snapped his fingers and the rest of the Brothers came forward to seize Willow, Sometimes and Essential.

'No!' cried Essential, who raised her hands to freeze him, but it didn't work. She kept on raising her hands. *Nothing happened.*

Willow swallowed.

'It's almost sweet how you believe that your magic would work on me – as if I hadn't ensured against that by using a protective spell the minute I allowed Moreg Vaine to step through these doors. Well –' Silas stroked the box of spells – 'I must admit that I have

265

enjoyed our time together – it felt good to finally tell the truth; it does release something inside. But enough of this. It is time to say goodbye now . . .'

Willow opened up the carpetbag as surreptitiously as she could, her hand searching as he spoke . . . Ybaer had said she'd know when the time was right and Willow did. From inside the carpetbag she grabbed hold of the stealth sprig and instantly disappeared.

'What on Great Starfell?' cried Silas.

Willow, realising that he couldn't see her, made her way slowly and carefully towards him.

She grabbed

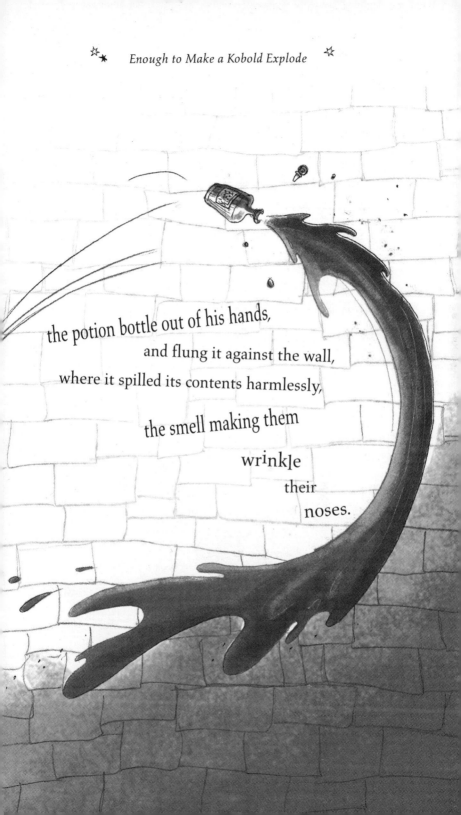

the potion bottle out of his hands,
and flung it against the wall,
where it spilled its contents harmlessly,

the smell making them

wrinkle

their

noses.

But all too soon she was visible again.

'Seize her!' cried Silas and one of the guards ran forward.

Essential raised her hands and froze the guard. Fortunately for them whatever spell Silas had used to protect himself against magic he obviously hadn't shared with his fellow Brothers.

'We've got maybe a second. Do something!' shouted Essential as the frozen Brothers stared at them with murder in their eyes.

Willow's eyes fell on the shaggy carpetbag. She stared at the greenish orange kobold, and thought hard. They said if you insulted a kobold enough . . . they would explode.

'Oswin, I have to tell you something before we die. I know that your father was a cat, and your mother wasn't really a kobold,' she lied.

'WOT?!'

He turned a bright pumpkin colour, his tail electrified in fury. His huge orb-like eyes blazing white-hot heat.

Willow spoke fast, choosing words that would upset him

most. 'A common tabby, wasn't she? And it was really just your grandmother who was a kobold . . . so you're not really, technically even a monster.'

'I AM **THE MONSTER** FROM UNDER THE BED!' he roared.

'NO, you're just a cat!'

'CAN A CAT DO THIS?'

he bellowed, just as the Brothers unfroze and raced towards them.

Willow threw the bag straight at them. 'Duck!' she told Essential and Sometimes.

There was a giant explosion.

Willow's hairy carpetbag burst apart with a bang, with Oswin glowing in the centre like a fireball. The roof caved in, and the Brothers went flying backwards.

There was an angry shout from Silas. 'Get them – get that girl!'

Abruptly a loud roar rent the air, and the floor began to shake. Something large, heavy and ferocious had landed on the already disintegrating roof. Bits of tile and plaster rained upon them from above. Amidst the falling debris Willow saw a dragon.

'Feathering!' she cried.

The dragon eyed them and said very calmly in his deep rumbly, windy voice, 'Afternoon . . . We had a feeling that you might be needing us?'

From behind his great wings she could see a slightly nervous-looking troll give a bashful sort of smile. Calamity. The troll was holding the hag stone, and said, 'Turns out Wolkana wasn't that far away; we saw it with this, and it helped us enter. Whatever magic protects this place doesn't work on hag stones!'

'Brilliant!' cried Willow.

A roof tile had clipped Silas on the head and a streak of blood trickled down his face. Despite this he lunged for Willow. 'Ignore them! Get the girl,' he commanded.

The remaining Brothers hesitated, so Silas went to Moreg Vaine's still body and took a knife from his cloak. He stared intently at Willow and said,

'Surrender or she dies here and now.'

Willow thought hard. In years to come she would still wonder at what she'd done, but she did the only thing she could. She closed her eyes, raised her hands to the sky and summoned the lost spell.

And *magic*, the magic of Starfell, sat up for a moment, as if it had been listening with one ear till then. And it drew closer to the small girl with hope in her chest, who was trying to fix things, and it decided to take a chance. And, to Willow's utter surprise, the spell flew out of the golden box, and landed in her outstretched hand with a purplish glow.

'You leave me no choice,' said Silas, and he stabbed Moreg beneath the ribs.

Willow watched as Moreg's blood pooled on her dusky robes, the colour draining from her face, all life trickling out of her.

'NO!' she shouted, racing towards the witch.

The pain from her wound woke Moreg up at last, but not for long – she was fading fast. Moreg gasped for breath. 'Do it, girl. Remember, *practical makes perfect.*'

Willow's lips trembled. 'B-but I can't.'

'Yes, you can, you know you can,' hissed the witch. 'Recite the counter-spell.'

Willow's eyes filled with tears as she watched Moreg's body start to shudder. Time was running out.

Willow took one last look at Moreg's body, tears coursing down her face, then she read the counter-spell on the scroll aloud as quickly as she could.

'What was taken now restore,

Put back what was lost before,

Return the day to its rightful space,

Time before time and past in place!'

A blast of silvery light knocked her off her feet, the scroll crumbled to dust in her hand, and suddenly everyone around her was spinning inside a reeling tornado.

She whirled passed Silas, his face dark and incredulous. Past Feathering, and Essential, Calamity, Oswin and Nolin Sometimes, and then suddenly it all went black, as black as night.

# 21

## Yesterday Again

She was in her cottage garden. There was a familiar crowd of people snaking along the low wall outside.

Willow blinked. What had happened? Why was she here? Where was Moreg? Nolin Sometimes? Feathering? Essential Jones?

In her confusion she heard skinny Ethel Mustard whine a strangely familiar whine. 'I heard witches weren't meant to ask for money in the first place . . . They're not meant to profit from their gifts,' she said.

Willow's mouth fell open. Hadn't this already happened? Her brain felt like a puddle of mush as she tried to make sense of what was happening. Through the fog she heard Juniper round on Ethel. 'Who told you that?'

Then slowly, painfully, and all at once the truth hit

her like a knife in her belly. She doubled over, gasping for breath, hot tears sliding down her face, as all the memories of the day that had been taken away came flooding back.

It was what she'd been fighting all along. What she'd known deep in her heart had to be true.

When she looked up, eyes glistening, she saw that everyone was wearing black, and, as if from a void, she heard Flora Bunton's reprimand. 'This isn't the time to be bringing up such a thing . . . We're here to show our support for the girls on this sad day as they say goodbye.'

Willow closed her eyes and her chin wobbled as she remembered it all . . . the day that Silas had taken away from her, from all of them.

*The day had started off like any other Tuesday. She got up, poked Oswin to stop his snores from under the bed, and then she got dressed in her pond-green dress, the one that bubbled in crooked lines at the hem because it had been sown by Granny Flossy's unsteady hands.*

*Breakfast was a slice of almost stale bread and a lick of her favourite jam and butter. Then she went outside*

to collect the eggs from the hens, which was when she saw Granny Flossy sitting in the garden chair outside. And suddenly, just like that, it was the saddest Tuesday of Willow's young life.

Granny Flossy's long green hair had winked in the morning light, and on the chair next to her sat her purple hat with its jaunty green feather. Granny's faded patchwork shawl had slipped from her shoulders on to the ground. Fallen out of her grasp too lay the old notebook, the one she recorded her latest potion experiments in, and on her face was a small smile, as if she were only just resting a while.

Willow stood with sobs choking her while she clutched at the old woman's hand, stroking her dear old cheek. She stayed that way for ages, before she finally went inside to tell her family what had happened . . .

Afterwards there'd been more tears . . . and the feeling that she may never be happy ever again, and when Willow got into bed that night she cried so hard that Oswin brought her every last thing that she'd ever made the mistake of saying that she liked, and, despite the smell, she hugged him close, and because she was very sad he let her. And while she sobbed Willow had wished with all her heart that it had never happened,

and somehow, though not because of that wish, but because of a spell cast very far away by a Brother of Wol, who was born with magic in his veins, what she had wanted most had come true.

Willow, like everyone else in Starfell, had woken up the next day without any memory of anything that had happened that fateful Tuesday. She was only left with a feeling of something sad tugging at the sleeve of her mind, trying to get her attention, something just out of her grasp.

The worst thing was that there was a tiny part of everyone's mind that must have known . . . because no one wondered where Granny Flossy was. No one thought it was strange that they hadn't seen her . . . Everyone had just gone back to their normal lives as if nothing had happened.

Willow had wondered, though. She'd sensed that there was something wrong, something missing, and while it would have been easier to just pretend that it hadn't happened she'd realised that it had been so much worse to forget.

But now it seemed like life had just reset itself, the way it should have been before the spell was cast.

It was three days after her grandmother had died. And Willow was now standing where she should have stood the day Moreg had come to find her, only now Moreg *wasn't* coming to find her. The trouble was that Willow remembered both versions. The week when Tuesday had gone missing and the week when it hadn't.

And just when Willow was wondering if she was the only one who remembered, if it was possible that the friends she had made didn't even remember her, an enormous blue dragon filled the sky, coming to land with a deafening thud just outside the low garden wall, shaking the entire hillside.

Around them people began to scream.

Ethel Mustard fainted.

'Feathering,' breathed Willow.

Willow's mother rushed forward, along with Juniper and Camille. 'Don't panic, don't panic,' she called. She was clearly panicking.

Feathering rolled a giant golden eye as Willow touched his silken, feathered face. 'Honestly, I'm a cloud dragon . . . Have they so little sense?' he asked Willow.

'Well, you are a *dragon*,' she said.

'This is true, young Willow.'

Camille gasped, her emerald-green eyes huge. 'He knows your name!'

Feathering shrugged a wing. 'Of course I do. It's her I've come to see,' he chided.

Willow's mother made a funny squeak.

Feathering ignored this. 'It worked – you did it, look,' he said, nodding his head towards the sky, where two dragons were approaching, one enormous and red, the other small and a pearly sort of blue, so much like his father.

'Oh!' She sniffed, wiping away a tear. 'He *hatched*.'

Feathering nodded. 'Thanks to you we thought, under the circumstances, we'd name him Floss – it seemed a good name – after your grandmother.'

Willow couldn't speak for the tears in her eyes and her chin started to wobble. 'I . . . thank you – she would be very honoured.'

Feathering's mate Thundera landed alongside the baby dragon, Floss, and she said, 'Feathering told me what you did – thank you.'

'It wasn't just me. I had a lot of help along the way.' She reached inside her pocket and felt inside something hard and flat, along with something sharp and hard, and pulled them out. It was the StoryPass

and the troll whistle. She grasped them tight, even though the edges of the whistle dug into her palm. She opened the StoryPass. Right then it was pointing to *There be Dragons*. And true enough, there were now three dragons in Willow's garden.

Floss was about the size of a bloodhound, and he butted her playfully as she stroked his head.

'We passed Calamity on the flight over . . . it seems that she was well and has been welcomed back into the clan.' Feathering cleared his throat. 'Despite the fact that she lost the battle with Verushka . . .'

'Oh . . .' Willow said, eyes wide. Then she smiled. 'That's wonderful news. I am so glad that they accepted her, even though she wasn't their usual sort

of troll.' Which Willow privately thought was a great thing.

Camille made a scared sort of noise.

'Help? T-trolls?' asked her mother, who seemed to have finally found her voice. 'What are they talking about? How did you help them?'

'Oh, it's a long story . . . and perhaps one day I'll tell it,' said Willow.

One time Willow might have wanted the glory, wanted her family to know what she'd done, for them to think, just once, that she was 'special' or 'important', but now she realised it didn't matter at all what they thought. What mattered was what she thought of herself.

When the dragons left, Camille gave her an odd look. 'Who knew being a magical bloodhound could have a plus side? I mean, the worst magical ability in the whole family, an embarrassment really – and yet a dragon—'

'Camille!' reprimanded Willow's mother sharply.

Willow shook her head. 'No, she's right. I can't blow things up or move things with my mind. What I do will never be grand or impressive, but what I've learnt about power is that we all have some.

282

It's not about how much you've got; it's about what you do with the little bit you have that matters most.'

There was a stunned silence.

'Are you all right?' asked Juniper.

'Yes,' said Willow. 'Or I will be. Actually, I've decided that you're right. I have decided to raise my price to a fleurie and a Leighton apple from now on. Please spread the word.'

There was a collective gasp all round. Willow had never increased her price *ever*.

Juniper's mouth opened and closed. 'Y-you are?' she said in surprise.

Willow nodded. Camille and her mother seemed nonplussed. She didn't try explaining herself. A fleurie was hardly a profit. Besides, as Moreg had said once, a witch's business was none but her own.

'Are you sure you are all right?' asked Juniper. 'It's just . . . you don't seem yourself?'

'What?' she asked, looking past Juniper for a face that wasn't there, hope furling inside her chest.

Juniper waved a hand in front of her. 'It's just that I've never really seen you place any value on your skills before – such as they are.'

283

'Well . . . today might be a good time to start,' said a voice.

Willow turned. And there she was.

A lone witch, tall and reed-thin, in dusky robes and pointed purple boots was just outside the garden gate. Her coal-black eyes twinkling with mild amusement.

'Is that Moreg Vaine?' cried Camille, her face white as a sheet.

Willow nodded. She could hear her sisters' knees knocking from here.

Moreg greeted them all, then pulled Willow aside. 'I'm so sorry about your grandmother.'

'Thank you,' said Willow.

'I knew, when I was asking you, that it would be hard, as you'd have to face it. I'm sorry for that; you were the only one who really had something to lose by finding the lost day.'

Willow looked down and fought back a tear. 'I know. It was easier not knowing, but at the same time it was so much worse. This way, no one forgets her, or what she did.'

Moreg nodded. 'I knew you were different.'

'They all think I'm a bit odd,' admitted Willow.

Moreg shrugged. 'The best people often are.'

Willow looked at her. 'But I remember everything – and so does Feathering, and you, why doesn't anyone else?'

'I think it's because we were all there in the presence of the spell, and so we remember both versions of the past.'

'So Calamity, Nolin Sometimes and Essential Jones will remember too?'

'They will,' agreed Moreg.

Willow was relieved. She liked the feeling that her new friends wouldn't forget her.

They're not the only ones who remember,' said Moreg, her face suddenly grave.

Willow frowned, then gasped. 'The Brothers of Wol and Silas – he will remember too.'

'Yes, we know his secret, which he won't be pleased about, but we'll be ready for him if he escapes the High Master again, which is why I've brought you this.'

Willow frowned as Moreg pulled out a broom from her new portal cloak and placed it along the wall.

A sleek beautiful broom that had white tail feathers mixed within the twigs. *Whisper.*

Then the witch gave her a hug, and raised a hand in farewell, or was it victory?

285

'I'll see you soon,' she said. And, as Willow's sisters gaped, their mouths wide, Moreg Vaine got on her own broom with its twin engines that roared into life, adjusted her flying goggles and shot up into the sky, leaving a trail of bright orange flames and Willow's

wild laughter

in her

wake.

# Acknowledgements:

Thank you to dearest Catherine Zamojski, who read the first instalments of Willow and her adventures, and used to ask for more. I'm not sure I would have carried on without your encouragement, especially in the beginning!

To my husband, Rui, for the inspiration behind Oswin's lexicon and silliness, and for being my (somewhat grumpy) best friend too.

To my gorgeous agent, Helen Boyle, who has made this a dream come true – thanks for all that you do!

Huge thank-you to my wonderful editor, Harriet Wilson. You have made this such a joy, and I have loved every minute.

To the incredible Sarah Warburton for bringing the world of Starfell to life and making me gasp with delight as each new illustration arrived – you are a dream come true.

To everyone at HarperCollins: Ann-Janine Murtagh, Rachel Denwood, Julia Sanderson, Margot Lohan, David McDougall, Sean Williams, Elorine Grant, Alex Cowan, Yasmin Morrissey, Beth Maher, Geraldine Stroud, Val Braithwaite – your enthusiasm, kindness and creativity has blown me away.

Thank you so much to my parents for your never-ending support and love. To my brothers, Simon and Dylan – while you may have been the inspiration behind Willow's remarkable sisters, unlike them you always made me feel very loved and cherished, despite me being the family geek.

Thank you as well to Odette, Joao, Didi, Gia, Ava, Claudia, Ben and the entire clan of Valentes and Bradleys, Kaplans and Watsons, and Van Wyks – I love you all.

A special thank-you to Granny Monica, who inspired Granny Flossy (minus the madness and green hair, of course!). You came into my life at just the time when I needed you and, like Willow, you made me feel special in my own way, and encouraged my lifelong love of books!

Finally – a big thank you to you, the reader, for taking a chance on Willow, and the world of Starfell. Thank you for coming on this adventure with me.